A Candlelight Ecstasy Romance™

HIS TOUCH SENT SHOCK WAVES OF PLEASURE COURSING THROUGH HER BODY. . . .

The touch of his fingers stroking her skin caused a tremor to pulsate across her nerves. His expertise tantalized her and made her long for him as she had never longed for a man before. He was a total stranger. He was a man she would never see again but for this one night. Yet he seemed made for her. Everything he did felt so good, so right. . . .

Masquerade
of Love

Alice Morgan

A CANDLELIGHT ECSTASY ROMANCE™

Published by
Dell Publishing Co., Inc.
1 Dag Hammarskjold Plaza
New York, New York 10017

Dell ® TM 681510, Dell Publishing Co., Inc.

Candlelight Ecstasy Romance™ is a trademark of
Dell Publishing Co., Inc., New York, New York.

ISBN: 0-440-15405-7

Printed in the United States of America
First printing—April 1982

Dear Reader:

In response to your continued enthusiasm for Candlelight Ecstasy Romances™, we are increasing the number of new titles from four to six per month.

We are delighted to present sensuous novels set in America, depicting modern American men and women as they confront the provocative problems of modern relationships.

Throughout the history of the Candlelight line, Dell has tried to maintain a high standard of excellence to give you the finest in reading enjoyment. That is and will remain our most ardent ambition.

> Anne Gisonny
> Editor
> Candlelight Romances

CHAPTER ONE

Brad Lucas frowned as he sat contemplating the drink set before him. Whiskey swirled around cubes of ice while the harassed bartender turned to mix another drink in the darkened lounge.

Live music resounded through the room, its seductive beat a reminder that he hadn't had a woman in seven months. It was his longest period of celibacy since attaining manhood in his middle teens.

As he sipped the fiery liquid his eyes caught the mirrored image of the band's lead singer. He looked without interest at her voluptuous figure exposed in a clinging black gown. She leaned forward, swaying with the tune, her husky voice and blatant words a deliberate attempt to excite the male audience.

Turned off by her overt sexuality, Brad shrugged. The taste of whiskey was as bitter as his thoughts as he emptied the glass in one swallow.

Boredom was his problem, he thought with ill humor. Three days of gambling, numerous beautiful women for the taking, yet he felt too jaded to receive joy from their expected mating ritual. Lies and false smiles were no longer worth the temporary physical release he received from their bodies.

The darkened bar, with its heavy layer of cigarette smoke, constant sight of gambling in the adjoining casino, and endless din of music played at deafening crescendos, gave him a sudden headache.

Placing a tip on the counter, he swiveled his seat around, preparing to leave, when he spotted the woman. Her appearance stopped him. He remained seated, elbows and back leaning against the padded edge of the bar. He watched her hesitate, her eyes searching the room, before she tilted her chin upward and walked toward the bar. Brad was stunned; his eyes narrowed as she came straight to him, her smile showing perfect white teeth vivid against glossy red lipstick.

"Are you saving this seat?" she asked, her soft voice breathless, her lashes lowered to shield the thoughts running through her mind.

"For you," he answered, turning to face her. All thought of leaving dismissed, Brad's face expressed welcome, despite annoyance at the sudden surge of desire filling his loins. A desire as unexpected as the approach of the beautiful young blonde asking to sit beside him.

He motioned for the bartender, a smile tugging his firm lips as he offered, "My name is Brad Lucas. What would you like to drink, Ms. . . ." Pausing, he waited for her to tell him her name.

"Brandy."

"Rather potent drink for a lady."

"No, that's my name. Brandy . . . Smith, to be exact," she explained, easing her hips onto the tall stool. Sitting to his right, fingers clasping her beaded evening purse with a tight grip, she glanced at him.

"I would like a screwdriver, please."

"Rather potent drink also." He smiled, then placed

their order before returning his eyes to the beauty of her features. She had wide eyes as amber as the brandy of her name, their irises ringed by a circle of black. Her eyes avoided contact with his for longer than a moment, but he had already been entranced by their velvety depths that waited to be explored by a man.

His gaze roamed slowly over her. She was exquisite: dark brows thinly plucked, thick sooty lashes, and a diminutive nose above a soft-looking, sensual mouth.

The only jarring feature was her hair: a mass of blond curls. The brassy color turned him off, since he was partial to brunettes, but he surmised it probably came from a bottle anyway. His eyes left her face to linger on each curve of her figure, aware she was watching him intently also.

Brandy's provocative actions were made easier by her intense desires and Brad's receptive behavior. Her hands shook around the icy glass as she nervously assessed the man she had chosen to be her partner for the night.

He is perfect, she told herself silently. *Unruly hair as black as Daniel's. Eyes the same smoke-gray.* After that their resemblance ended. Brad was a towering man, his presence attracting her the minute she entered the lounge.

His broad shoulders were outlined by the perfect cut of a black dress suit, his white shirt immaculate against the deep tan of his throat and hands. She could see the muscles in his thighs tauten as her gaze swept over the length of his body, ending at the elegant black shoes hooked casually over the barstool bracing.

Brad was curious at the intensity of his interest. It seemed strange that Brandy's shapely figure covered in soft black fabric from throat to knee, shoulder to wrist, was so sensual. Much more than the exposed curves of the

9

blond singer whose pendulous breasts threatened to slip out of her dress top each time she leaned forward. Brandy was a small girl, her fine-boned slender legs and strappy sandals with spike heels bringing her no taller than his heart.

He wanted to know more about her. Somehow she didn't fit the pattern of the usual bar pickup. The haunted look in her eyes bothered him. It was wary, even desperate. Damn, she was beautiful. He wanted her with a sudden wild, primitive lust.

"Is this your first visit to Las Vegas?" he asked in a low voice, seemingly interested in her answer.

"No. I've been here many times," she answered truthfully. She fidgeted with her glass, inhaling when she felt his hand grip her fingers to still their movement.

She felt alarmed by the excitement at his touch, but she forced herself to allow the contact. She had not planned on awareness or physical magnetism between herself and the man she selected. It was an unexpected distraction that added to the trauma she would be forced to endure later that night. She remained silent, watching as Brad took his finger and ran it across the back of her hand, feeling pleasure despite his being a stranger.

With ease from years of experience in social contact Brad stroked her hand before sliding to her ring finger. He touched the indentation where her wedding ring had circled for five years.

He knows, she cried inwardly as his hand clasped hers, turning it palm-side up before looking at her, his expression serious.

"Married?"

Unable to answer because of a catch in her throat, Brandy bowed her head, shaking it no.

10

Always careful to avoid involvement with a married woman, Brad sensed she was lying. Dammit he thought. If her old man couldn't keep her satisfied, why the hell should he hesitate to try? Brad's body hardened just at the thought of taking her to bed, physical arousal an emotion he hadn't felt in too long and one he wanted to appease.

"Alone in Vegas?"

"Yes. Are you?" Her brassy blond hair shone in the glimmer from the bar as she turned to smile at him.

His breath caught at the flawless beauty of her face as he returned her smile. "Very much so, and it's a fact I now find unbearable. Will you dance with me?"

Brandy set her drink on the bar and started to step to the floor, only to feel her waist grasped in his hands, the length of his fingers spanning its narrow width easily.

"You are large, Brad," she commented, her head barely reaching his shoulder. "I've never danced with anyone this tall."

"Don't worry about it, little one. If I find I can't avoid your toes, I'll lift you right off the ground. You're petite enough to fit into one of my pockets."

"Hardly," she whispered. "Could we dance without talking? I'd like to let the beat of the music completely block out my thoughts."

She turned into his arms with ease, her body fitting his sensuously, despite the difference in their heights. Without coyness or teasing she lay against him, her body supple against his taut contours as they danced slowly around the crowded floor.

Her figure was more voluptuous than he had expected. He could feel the fullness of her breasts as she clung to his neck. Crossing his hands behind her back, he pulled her closer, inhaling the heady scent of her expensive perfume.

Thankful that she found a man like Brad and that her encounter was successful, Brandy clung to his neck, her face resting directly over his heart. The material of his suit was smooth against her cheek, though she found his great size intimidating. His commanding presence seemed to engulf her, the magnetism of his masculinity aroused her senses.

His heady after-shave was woodsy, unlike Daniel's, but more to her liking. With tenacious will she forced her mind away from anything beyond the moment, an accomplishment made easier by the plush casino's impersonal environment and the compelling stranger whose steps she followed with ease.

Aware of her desire for silence, Brad was content to dance. His intrigue mounted as she relaxed. He cupped her hips, holding them firmly to his body before his hands lifted to fondle her back. Her continued submission increased his libido with alarming speed.

Wanting the warmth of Brad's hard male body, Brandy let the passion he awoke magnify without restraint. Her surrender to his physical presence satisfied a deep need, the need for security through male dominance and possession. She was unaware that a man could kindle such fierce yearning in a woman. Her heart raced madly, her stomach tying in knots, when his chin lowered to rest against her forehead.

Their bodies swayed in time to the incessant beat of the band. Brad's increasing desire was obvious but not objectionable. His purpose could not be served unless she attracted him.

Brandy could feel Brad's mouth open, kissing her forehead before moving across her brow. Raising her face, she smiled with encouragement, shivering at the lazy look of

12

sensuous pleasure in his smoky eyes. She stroked his wide shoulders while his fingers continued to play along her spine.

His eyes softened, mouth teasing across her brow before lowering to nibble the edge of her mouth. "Mmm . . . you taste delicious."

Brad's warm breath and husky voice were as stimulating as his touch. Brandy could feel her breasts swell as she squirmed to get closer, her sensitive nipples hardening against the pressure of his broad chest moving back and forth as they danced. With parted lips she took his kiss, allowing him to deepen the lengthy caress until he was forced to stop.

Brad inhaled twice before abruptly leaving the floor to guide her back to the bar. He ordered drinks, a stall for time, as he attempted to understand why she ignited his senses.

Shaken by the stirring contact of his intimate kiss, Brandy sought to relieve the tension. "Do you have a cigarette, Brad?" She was stunned. He hadn't asked for a kiss—just took her lips until her mind had blocked out everything but his touch.

He took a cigarette case out of his breast pocket and, removing a cigarette for her, watched her reaction with curiosity. Their hands touched as she reached for it. She placed the filtered tip between her lips, then bent to touch it to the lighter. The solid-gold case and lighter were as elegant as their owner.

She inhaled sharply before breaking into a spasm of coughing. Brad removed the cigarette from her, crushing it in the ashtray before pinning her with his eyes. "Obviously you don't smoke, do you?"

Recovered from the sudden coughing, she looked at

him. "Not a very good attempt to act sophisticated, was it?"

"No . . . nor does smoking make you sophisticated. The moment you walked into the bar, your demeanor put every woman here to shame. You walk like a queen, Brandy, and you are the most exquisite woman I have ever seen."

Brandy lowered her lashes, refusing to meet his eyes. His tone was serious when he complimented her. She liked his strong profile and taut throat. His nose was straight, mouth sensual and warm, chin firm. The handsome ruggedness pleased her femininity. His well-shaped head was crowned with shimmering pitch-black hair, its vibrant thickness free of spray or oils.

Brad sat without comment, sipping his whiskey, aware that Brandy was watching him. His blood ran hot, bringing out latent savagery. God, he wished he were inside her, making her respond to his desires. He checked his watch and was surprised to discover that it was only two o'clock in the morning. Plenty of time left to seduce her here.

Las Vegas was a town that never slept. Unless a person went outside, it was often impossible to tell if it was day or night.

His muscles tightened as Brandy crossed her legs, her dress skirt hiking up to reveal several inches of nylon-clad thigh.

Finished with her drink, Brandy turned to him. With no warning or prior nervousness she held his glance, asking, "Brad . . . would you like a woman tonight?"

He was stunned by her request, but he finished his drink slowly, and casually set the glass on the counter before swiveling to face her.

"You?" he asked enticingly.

14

"Yes," she whispered, darkened lashes forming crescents on her cheeks as they lowered. Brandy stiffened, waiting for his answer, afraid he would turn her down.

He watched her, his gray eyes darkening as his brain reeled with the bluntness of her request. Could she have read his mind?

"No fit man in the world could turn down an offer from you."

"I only want you, Brad," she answered truthfully, refusing to tell him just how incorrect his statement was—that in actuality many men would not want her.

"If you're serious, then let's go to my suite. I see no reason to waste further time in a bar."

Repressing her fear, she took her purse, smiling at him as she stepped down from the stool.

Brad's hand clasped Brandy's waist possessively as he led her from the lounge. Dazed by her approach, her abrupt request for him to make love to her, he guided her to the casino's private elevators.

Reserved for high-rollers, the upper suites were luxurious enough to please the most wealthy and discriminating patron. A room befitting the man who occupied it. The noiseless elevator stopped at the top floor, opening to reveal a carpeted hall and several wide doors discreetly closed.

Brad unlocked the closest, guiding her inside by the elbow. Brandy looked over the huge living room area, impressed by the elegant decor, before returning her gaze to Brad. She watched his shoulder muscles ripple beneath the fine silk of his shirt as he shrugged out of his jacket.

He tossed it carelessly on the back of the broad couch before turning to ask, "Do you want a drink or something to eat? I'll call down for anything you wish that isn't here."

Dropping her purse on top of his jacket, Brandy silently walked forward. She stood before him and placed a hand on each side of his face, the lean planes of his cheeks taut, a faint stubble shadowing the deeply tanned skin. Raised on tiptoes, she touched his mouth in a light kiss.

"I want nothing, Brad . . . but your love."

The months of celibacy took a toll on Brad's control and he pulled her into his arms. His hard mouth took her lips in a brutal kiss as he bent her to the curve of his body. Momentarily unconcerned for her physical comfort he ravaged her with a hungry caress. He expected a protest, but instead, he felt her lips part, the moist sweetness within offered without question as she touched the tip of his tongue with her own.

Overpowered by the scent of her body, her willing response, he crushed her breasts against his chest, his broad palm pressed beneath her shoulder blades to be sure she didn't move away. The thin material of his shirt was no barrier, as he felt her nipples harden, their erotic touch a further stimulant to his overheated senses.

Brandy let the expertise of Brad's mouth incite her passions, offering no protest when he swung her into his arms. Their lips clung as he walked forward to the vast bedroom, where the center of attraction was a mammoth bed mounted on a raised platform.

Brad stopped, his mouth lifting so they could catch their breath. His broad chest rose and fell rapidly as he watched the velvety depths of her eyes darken. The excitement that was generated on first contact was equally intensified.

Pulling from his hold, Brandy looked around the room.

She watched without comment as Brad switched off the overhead light. The dim bedside lamp softened the effect of the blatantly sexual decor but added to the intimacy between them. The maid had already turned back the spread to expose satin sheets in startling black, a sharp contrast to the spread of lustrous alpaca fur in soft beige shades.

Brad pulled the tie from his collar and with deft fingers started to unbutton his shirt. He stopped when he noticed Brandy slip off her sandals.

"Do you want to undress me?" she asked, appearing small and fragile in the large room.

"Not this time. I think I prefer to sit here and watch you do it." Brad sat down in the deep bedside chair, leaning back to watch her reaction. His eyes narrowed as, undaunted, she removed her dress, careful to lay it neatly over the silk lounge chair beside her.

Clad in a black silk full slip, she stood before him, her glance taking in his outstretched legs. His well-shaped hands with short-clipped fingernails rested on the chair arms in a relaxed manner. As she started to turn her back his voice halted her.

"Don't, Brandy. Face me. Let me see all of you."

Unembarrassed, she faced him, her eyes locking with his for a long moment before taking the hem of her slip and pulling it over her tightly curled hair.

She heard his brief exclamation of pleasure as her body was exposed to his gaze. The deep-cut underwire bra of black lace barely concealed the beauty of her full breasts. A lace garter belt held up sheer nylons of a light tan shade. Hip-hugging panties matched the dainty bra. The dark sensual underwear contrasted vividly with her creamy skin, emphasizing its flawless beauty.

Within seconds she had rolled down her hose, removed the garter belt, and placed them neatly on her dress. His eyes darkened to deep smoldering charcoal when he saw her hands raise to unclip her bra. With graceful movements she eased it from her body, the perfection of her high breasts filling his body with desire so strong, he had to force himself to remain seated.

Brad ached with a sudden primitive male need to conquer. He wanted to plunder each curve, each hidden recess, with his mouth and hands until she begged him to release her sexual tensions.

She raised her slender shapely legs one at a time as she slipped off the last of her dainty underwear. Her full breasts were firm as she bent forward, the nipples enticing rosy pink buds.

My God, he moaned to himself. The sight of her was enough to make a man go mad with anticipation. Her clothing was fragile and obviously costly, but to see her nakedness he would tear it to shreds.

Brandy stood before him, her chin tilted proudly, fully aware that her slim body was totally exposed in the soft light. She could feel his desire. It reached across the room like a magical spell, binding them together with an illusion of love.

Brad's eyes lingered on each curve; he was amazed that the tiny creature before him could have such a stunning impact on his sensuality. He had had many women through the years, gorgeous women experienced in the arts of erotic pleasure, but never had one perfect bit of femininity aroused in him such deep hunger. Just looking at Brandy brought his desire to a dangerous pinnacle.

The husky timbre of his voice echoed in the room as he

commanded, "Come to me, Brandy. Come let me love you until we're both mindless with the wonder of it all."

As graceful as a ballet dancer she came forward. Hands outstretched, head held proudly, she stopped at his feet. Thick sooty lashes fluttered to conceal her thoughts from his piercing gaze. Fiery glints smoldered in their darkened depths.

Unable to restrain the desire to hold her in his arms any longer, Brad stood, his hands reaching for her shoulders. The first touch of her satiny naked skin was his undoing. He pulled her to him, raising her upward to meet his demanding mouth as his head lowered to claim her lips.

Brandy raised her hands to clasp his nape, her breasts crushed against the hair-roughened skin of his wide chest bared by his unbuttoned shirt. She felt her body quiver as he parted her lips to seek the warmth, his tongue touching hers avidly. The fervor of his passion seared her as he plundered her mouth. He groaned huskily, as if crazed by her taste and unrestrained response.

Meeting each demand, Brandy felt her mind whirl, her nerves sensitized by Brad's sexual expertise. His hands moved over her back and hips freely as he continued the caress.

Breathless at the assault on her emotions, she murmured softly against his lips, "Please slow down. I—I can hardly breathe."

Brad raised his head, chest heaving rapidly, mouth trailing across her face to the sensitive skin of her neck. He laughed huskily in agreement, his hands trembling across her back.

"You're very aptly named, my beauty. If man could distill a brandy as potent as your touch, no one would drink anything else. You are smooth as silk, one-hundred-proof dynamite and habit-forming after only one taste. I could devour you tonight, Brandy. Are you prepared to meet my needs?"

Placing a kiss in the hollow of his throat, she raised her eyes. Her voice was as evocative as a potent aphrodisiac to his senses as she whispered, "Yes, Brad. Without reservations. You lead and I'll follow."

"Oh, God, Brandy, you're really asking for it. But you're so damn small. I don't want to hurt you, little one. I'll try to be gentle"—his body shuddered—"but that's the furthermost desire from my mind."

Abruptly he swung her into his arms and carried her to the bed. With surprising tenderness Brad lay her on the sheets. She looked at him as he stood beside the bed, a soft smile tugging his lips. ·

"You're beautiful, Brandy. So exciting . . . so damn sensual! It will be a joy to savor each delectable curve of your body." His voice deepened to a harsh moan. "Of all the men alone in the bar . . . that you should pick me to be your partner is staggering!"

Brad removed his shirt as Brandy watched him with curious eyes. His hands unsnapped the waistband of his slacks, and he stepped out of them casually. His shoulders were wide, his chest powerful and hairy, his torso lean and fit. She watched, free of shame, as he slipped off his brief Jockey shorts before lowering himself to lie beside her. Her pulse began to beat unevenly, her limbs shivered.

Pale creamy skin shone against the dark linens as he raised his hands to thread his fingers through the brassy curls. Brandy's hands caught his as he touched her hair, stopping his exploration.

"Remove it!" Brad commanded, his face lowering to blow softly against the rapidly beating pulse of her throat.

"No, Brad . . . please," she protested weakly.

"Remove it now or I will. When I make love to a woman, I make love to all of her, and I don't want to run my fingers through any damn wig!" Leaning sideways on one elbow, he watched as she sat up.

Brandy removed the bobby pins she had used to secure the wig before pulling the blond mass of artificial curls from her head. Without self-consciousness she ran her fingers through her own hair tucked up tightly beneath. Long shimmery strands in dark chestnut-brown fell about her shoulders, their lustrous texture as silky as her skin. Gleaming color contrasted with the fairness of her shoulders as her hair fell in tumbled waves when she bent sideways to look at him.

"So much for my disguise." She shrugged, watching as he lay on his back, hands crossed beneath his neck, to scrutinize the remarkable change in her appearance.

"A lousy one too. You're even more beautiful now. Have I told you brunette is my favorite hair color?"

"No . . . but that's not important to us, is it, Brad? There's only one reason I'm here, and you know what that is."

"I thought I did but now I'm not so certain." His right arm snaked out to pull her across his chest. "Enough talk, Brandy."

His hand threaded through her hair, reveling in the silken strands, as he forced her down to meet his lips. With gentleness he searched her mouth, his lips playing with hers to bring them both heady satisfaction. God, he could kiss her for days.

His left hand trailed over her body, enjoying the feel of her satin-smooth skin as she lay across his broad chest, her soft abdomen resting over the hardness of his lean hips.

21

Wanting to extend their coming together, Brad savored each moment with Brandy in his arms. They clung together on the bed, her passion increasing with the gradual discovery of her body's needs.

Brad rolled her onto her back and leaned lightly across her, the weight of his body supported by his elbows. The velvety depths of her eyes lured him to continue, her expression reproached him for stopping.

He sat up, starting to leave the bed, when she touched him, her hand caressing the dark hair that covered his forearm.

"Don't leave me, Brad."

"I have to protect you. I hadn't planned on this tonight. They're in the bathroom. . . ."

"No, Brad. You don't need anything. I'm . . . on the . . . pill."

Returning to her side, he gathered her to him, taking her lips in long drugging kisses before descending to worship the mature curves of her breasts. The moist, surging movement of his mouth and sensual flicking of his tongue across her nipples caused them to harden into taut peaks.

The pleasure sent shock waves of intolerable need through her, increasing as his possession became more intimate. The touch of his fingers stroking her naked skin caused a tremor to pulsate across her nerves. His expertise tantalized her flesh, made her long for his touch, despite his being a veritable stranger—a man she would never see but for this one traumatic coupling. Everything he did felt so good and somehow right.

Suddenly caught in overpowering desire, overcome by the need for physical release, she pressed herself to him, her arms winding around his neck with surprising strength.

She clung to his head, holding him to her body, her fingers threading through his unruly hair. Her hips raised to meet his body as he covered her, his knees spreading her thighs.

Cupped beneath his aroused body, she could feel a damp film of perspiration break out on his skin when she reached to clasp his back. The fresh clean male smell of him invaded her nostrils, and a murmur of desire came spontaneously from the depth of her throat.

Raining fervent kisses along his neck, she knew the time had come to give her body to him—an act she never thought would be executed with a stranger. His hands were touching her freely, running over her limbs and breasts in tantalizing strokes. In a pleading voice she begged him to release her from the torment of his sensual onslaught.

"Take me, Brad! Give me your love now."

"Yes, Brandy . . . yes!" he gasped, his voice slurred with the passion she could feel beneath her fingertips as she continued to stroke his back.

She raised to accept his masculinity as he thrust against her, only to stop with an abruptness that was shocking in its speed.

"What the hell . . . ?" Pulling from her, he sat up and swung his legs over the side of the bed. He turned his head and his narrowed eyes pinned her, his body taut with anger, his chest heaving as he attempted to control his peaked desire.

"Tell me what game you're playing, Brandy. Is this some kind of sensuous masquerade?"

Face flushed with embarrassment, she reached out to him. "Of course not! It's not a game, Brad. I asked you to love me, and I haven't changed my mind."

She rose from the bed, her hands grasping his waist as she leaned into the nakedness of his broad back. Her voice was muffled as she pressed her face to his velvety tanned skin. His muscles were hard as steel and they rippled at her touch.

Pulling from her grasp, he stood up to face her, hands clenched alongside his hips, uncaring of his aroused nudity.

"Good God, this is the damnedest situation I've ever been in. I thought I was giving you the loving your husband wouldn't. I talked myself into taking a married woman for the first time in my life. What do I find instead but a virgin? Right now I'm not certain which is worse!"

"I told you I wasn't married," she answered calmly. "My virginity shouldn't matter to you, Brad. It's my body, and if I want you to be the first, I have the right to do so. I'm twenty-six and am a legal-age consenting adult."

Unable to believe what was happening, Brad sat back down on the bed and looked at her as she knelt on the sheets, her eyes beseeching him to love her.

"I've never taken a virgin before," he whispered in a husky voice. As he reached out to touch her cheek his hands trembled with the force of his desire.

"I've never had a man before, so it's a first for both of us." With tears streaming down her face she reached out for him, soft hands clinging to his neck as she threw herself into his arms.

Gently he lowered Brandy to the bed and kissed her, but his kisses had changed: they were no longer plundering, but persuasive, his own needs now tightly held in check. His hands were gentle as his desire for sex changed to a need to make love, to give pleasure as well as take it. It was the first time in his life a woman had aroused such tender, protective feelings. He felt vulnerable, humbled by her innocence.

With reverence he guided her through the traumatic denouement until she could accept his body without pain and could meet the pleasure of his thrusting masculinity with that equal to the gratification he felt with his body inside her.

In a quivering apex of sensuality they reached a climax so volatile, Brandy thought her heart would stop. Brad had driven all thoughts of the past from her mind after the first intimate touch of his hands. His taking of her virginity was so beautiful, she knew that his face, the eroticism of his touch, would be imprinted on her mind from that moment on. The feel of his body shuddering over her filled her heart with tenderness, his concern for her inexperience an insight to his inherent thoughtfulness and compassionate personality.

Cradled within Brad's arms, Brandy lay facing him, relaxing in the aftermath of a coming together so intense, the world could have ended and she wouldn't have cared. The warmth of his love flooded her. The sensual pleasure she had received was as unexpected as her longing to press against his length until he took her again.

Unconcerned by the reasons for her yearning desires, she rained fervent kisses on his throat and chest as his gentle hands leisurely stroked her back. Her need to continue touching him was overpowering.

The bliss of Brad's hands trailing across her skin, petting her with slow, languorous strokes before reaching to thread his fingers through her dampened curls was her first gratification. His passionate, virile lovemaking was what her virtuous body had unconsciously craved during the last five years.

Reaching upward, she pulled his head closer and kissed him on the mouth as an expression of sudden caring. Unbidden tears slipped beneath her tightly clenched lashes before she brought her shattered emotions under control. She could feel Brad's body harden at her touch and knew again the magic of awakening desire.

Brad's muscles tautened, overcome by an unbridled surge of longing to take her again. He rolled her onto her back, and his eyes lingered on her dreamy expression as his hands cupped her face gently.

"Was it good for you, Brandy? Did I give you pleasure too?" His voice was deep, his expression one of great tenderness.

Brandy raised her arms, bringing him to her eagerly, unashamed to reveal the enjoyment she received from his touch.

"It was beautiful, Brad. I can't describe how complete I feel now. How fulfilled—"

"You're gorgeous," he said, interrupting her. "It feels so good loving you. To let my passion explode within you—"

His words of passion and need were broken off when he took her mouth. Time stood still as again he guided her into the elementary pleasures of loving.

Brandy responded to his teaching, delighting in each new erotic pleasure until unknowingly crying out his name in her second tumultuous climax. Her first love had been bestowed with infinite generosity. Held possessively in his arms, she lay satiated, content in the silence of complete rapport.

Brad fell into a deep sleep, knowing Brandy was his first love, equally cherishing the knowledge that he was her only lover.

CHAPTER TWO

Brandy listened to Brad's even breathing. He was sound asleep, and she knew it was time to leave. Secure in the comfort of his arms, she placed a reverent, featherlight kiss across his lips.

"Thank you, Brad, for being my partner tonight. The temporary oblivion and physical fulfillment were like a miracle. May God forgive me for using you so treacherously," she whispered, her poignant plea barely audible in the silent room.

Careful not to disturb him, she eased away from the weight of his arms, arms that continued to hold her possessively despite his deep sleep. She drew the sheet up, covering his naked form before walking to her clothes.

Brandy's nerves were taut, fingers fumbling with haste as she put on her dress. She prepared to leave, standing barefoot, holding her sandals in her hand. Unable to control her sudden desire, she walked to the bed, wanting one last glance at Brad's strong masculine face.

Tears streamed unchecked down her cheeks as she watched him sleep. They were tears of regret that their relationship could never be permanent and had not been allowed time to develop slowly. Her breast ached that it was impossible to seek his love, not just the devastating consequences of his ardent, skillful lovemaking.

Brad's arm moved, hand outstretched, as if searching for her body, and a small moan escaped his lips. Fearful he would notice her absence from the bed, Brandy grabbed her evening purse and fled the suite, wary he might wake and follow. Once she was safely enclosed in the private elevator, she exhaled with relief. As it descended silently to the lobby she slipped into her sandals. When it stopped, the doors opening to reveal the continued din of the vast gambling casino, she paused and breathed deeply, then walked across the foyer, chin raised proudly, forcing the irrational behavior of the last few hours from her mind. The air was cold on her face as she stepped from the entryway, a glimpse of pitch-black sky barely visible with the millions of lights flickering along the famed Las Vegas strip.

Her hair glistened a deep brunette, hanging in tumbled waves around her shoulders as she hailed a taxi to take her down the strip to Caesars Palace, where she was staying. Within minutes she had entered the rented suite and for the second time that night undressed.

She walked into the bathroom, intent on taking a cold shower, hopeful the spray would cool her heated blood. The tingling spray brought her out of her reverie with a shock. She forced back tears by shutting her lids tightly, her emotions turbulent. "Your loving was perfect . . ." she whimpered, bemused.

She took a deep breath in the hope of steadying her nerves, while running the soft washcloth over her skin. The thought of the intimacy of her union with Brad brought a flush to her face. Her tender skin was still sensitive from his vigorous lovemaking despite his care not to hurt her. She doubted if he left a single bruise or mark on her body. Her own uninhibited actions and passionate response to a total stranger would have to be faced later when her emotions were under better control.

Anxious to leave Las Vegas, Brandy hurried with her shower, dried her body carelessly, then returned to the bedroom for her clothes. The black dress, beaded purse, evening sandals, and wispy lace slip and garter belt were neatly folded and zipped into the folds of a small canvas duffel bag.

Dressed in faded denim jeans, turtleneck sweater, leather jacket, and tennis shoes, she left the room. A silk scarf completely covered the vibrant color of her hair, and wide-framed dark glasses hid her teary eyes as she walked unnoticed from the foyer of Caesars.

Climbing into the backseat of the waiting taxi, she asked the driver to take her to the Greyhound bus depot. She checked her watch, breathing a sigh of relief. In fifteen minutes she would be aboard the bus, traveling anonymously back to her home.

Other than Brad, not another living soul would know she had left California, much less be aware she had given her virginity to an unknown man within two hours of their first meeting.

"Your bus is here, miss," the sleepy clerk explained, wondering why a young girl who couldn't even afford a decent outfit would come to Las Vegas. Probably lived here, he thought, and like most of the residents never entered a casino unless they worked there.

With a brief thank-you Brandy boarded the bus after handing the uniformed driver her ticket. It was crowded with people trying to sleep, as they traveled in the dark

29

early-morning hours. She walked along the aisle, finding an empty seat at the back.

She sat next to the window and placed her duffel bag on the adjoining seat, hoping no one would sit beside her. The last thing she could bear would be a well-meaning person wanting to converse. The six-and-a-half-hour trip to Pasadena would be torment enough without being bothered by a stranger wanting to make small talk.

The flight from Ontario to Las Vegas, which she traveled as a sophisticated blonde, had taken only forty-five minutes but to be sure that she couldn't be traced she decided that returning on the bus dressed as a transient would be wiser.

She lay her head against the high seat back, utterly exhausted. Eyes closed, hands clasped on her lap, she sought forgetfulness. The heavy drone of the bus's motor directly behind her, plus the rolling motion as they sped along the highway, released the last of her anxiety. Twenty-four sleepless hours took their effect on her and she slept deeply.

The piercing cry of a restless young child woke her, and tears filled Brandy's eyes, streaming down her cheeks unchecked. The ache for her baby daughter was unbearable, the hurt in her breast a constant reminder of her loss. Her empty arms were an agonizing void as painful as the deepest wound.

Brandy watched the sun rise, fingers clutching convulsively in her lap as she tried to regain control. Resting her forehead on the cold glass of the tinted windows, she showed no interest as traffic picked up in San Bernardino County. After a routine stop in Los Angeles the bus finally headed toward her hometown.

She grabbed the duffel bag, filing out with the other

passengers. She walked straight to the ladies' restroom and changed into the clothes she would wear home. With a shock at her carelessness she remembered leaving her blond wig in Brad's suite, the brassy curls a fluffy mass on the bedroom floor. Fortunately her name wasn't inside to identify her, but it was still a foolish error.

Wearing the dressy black outfit, she packed her casual clothes back in the canvas bag. She walked from the depot to the parking lot, where she had left her car the previous afternoon before taking a taxi to the airport.

With a sigh of relief she settled into the comfort of her own automobile. She looked like a young sophisticate used to the things wealth could provide as she eased her new Porsche from the lot. Her car was custom painted, its deep color identical to the brunette of her hair. Silky strands blew away from her forehead as she sped toward her home. The open window allowed the fresh air to cool her brow, bracing her for the confrontations ahead. The powerful motor hummed as she geared down to enter the concrete drive fronting her godfather's old Pasadena mansion. She parked in the rear breezeway and walked to the back-entrance door, leaving the duffel bag behind the seat.

"Good morning, Gracie," she greeted the housekeeper. A new employee, she had been in charge for only a few months but appeared to be excellent and was appreciated for her unobtrusive management.

"Good day, Mrs. Harcourt. Did you get all your business in Marina del Rey taken care of?"

Looking at Gracie's trim figure in the pale gold uniform, her short grayish hair, her unadorned narrow face and thin mouth, Brandy wondered if her sixty years had ever been touched with passion. Aware of how much her own feelings had changed overnight, Brandy hoped the housekeeper had experienced the tumultuous power of a man's sensual-interest. The memories might brighten the drabness of her life-style now.

"Yes, Gracie. Everything was easier than I thought it would be," she answered, pausing as she contemplated her lie.

"Well, I can certainly understand why, Mrs. Harcourt. Selling the condominium to your husband's law partner should have made the escrow contract easier for you. Maybe now you won't have to go back to the beach. It's best, I think, to stay away from places that make us sad. Losing your husband and child so tragically only three weeks ago is such a terrible shame. Why I—"

Brandy didn't like her problems discussed by the staff, so she abruptly changed the subject. Their sympathetic glances and attempts to baby her had not helped lessen the grief. She was appreciative of their concern but preferred to mourn the loss in the privacy of her room.

"Where's James?"

"He went to La Jolla to pick up the colonel. Scripps Hospital called, his tests were finished, and they felt it best if he return to his home. He was raising so much trouble, wanting to get back here, his blood pressure began acting up. Losing his only son and granddaughter has set him back." Noticing the sudden whiteness of Brandy's face, the housekeeper cooed, "Oh, my dear. I'm so sorry. Please forgive me. You're so composed all the time and concerned about the colonel's health that I forget about your grief." Clucking her tongue, she added solemnly, "Such a shame."

"That's all right, Gracie," Brandy murmured, desperately holding back tears. "I hope the colonel's heart wasn't damaged any further. I had to insist or he would never have considered having a complete checkup." She turned away from her housekeeper's curious eyes, annoyed by her own dwindling composure. "I'm going to my room."

Brandy walked through the large sunny kitchen. Modernized several times since the home was built in the early 1930s, it was fitted with every modern convenience and kept spotlessly clean. She ascended the wide stairway to her private suite of rooms in the west wing of the old rambling two-story house.

Inside, Brandy latched the door securely before kneeling beside the double bed. Head bowed, she huddled on the deep carpeting, her hands cradling her face as she began to cry. The pain became unbearable as she realized she couldn't stop. For the first time in twenty-one days she let the tears fall freely, their healing powers nearly as fulfilling as Brad's masculine security and gentle comfort as he caressed her after they made love.

She prayed for forgiveness for what she had done. Dismayed at the deviousness of her sudden scheme, she was aware that at that very moment her body could be nurturing the seed of another child. A child of her flesh that could replace the one she had lost. A child she needed desperately if she was to retain her sanity in the barren years ahead.

A second marriage was out of the question. The trip to Las Vegas had been a sudden brainstorm. A reckless attempt to conceive a replacement for the child taken so cruelly from her.

Brandy knew it was biologically the time she was most apt to get pregnant. There was never doubt in her mind that Brad could father a child. His very essence exuded overt sexuality. It was incomprehensible that he wasn't a virile, vigorous male.

Several minutes passed as she regained her composure before rising to walk to her private bathroom. Its soft green fitments were as feminine as the fragile gilded furniture in her bedroom.

She took a leisurely bath in a tub filled with her favorite essence. The warmth of the water was a soothing balm to her body.

Refreshed, hair brushed, fresh makeup applied, she felt more relaxed than she had in months. A hot flush tinged her cheeks at the realization that it was because of Brad. His tempestuous lovemaking had carried her into ecstasy and eased the tensions of the previous five years.

Within hours of meeting Brad she felt, for the first time, the release that a man's tender concern could bring to a woman. He showed her undreamed-of plateaus of sensuality before releasing her frustrations in blissful satisfaction. Brandy knew it would be impossible to forget him. If her plan succeeded, she would have his child—a constant reminder of her indiscretion and brief one-night affair.

Dressed in brown and gold plaid slacks and a soft gold cashmere sweater, Brandy relaxed on her bedroom lounge, waiting for her godfather to arrive. It was impossible to think of the kind old man who had raised her from the age of seven as anything other than her godfather, though he had also been her father-in-law since her marriage to Daniel.

She heard the neighbors' noisy Great Dane's bark. From the upstairs window she watched James drive the big Cadillac limousine into the driveway. The car's black paint was as glistening as the chrome: despite its age James kept it as bright as new. It was a plush, comfortable car, and her godfather saw no reason to change it. He refused to travel in anything else, most often seated in the vast

34

backseat by himself. James, wearing a peaked cap and dark uniform, sat as proud as the colonel in the driver's seat.

The colonel had never allowed Brandy to chauffeur him. He refused to ride in her smaller Porsche, not liking its low carriage and bucket seats. A regal old man with a mind of steel, he never deviated from a single decision once it was made.

As a retired Marine Corps colonel, he possessed commanding, arrogant leadership qualities, which had made him a formidable parent to his only son. He had not married until he was forty-five, and his young wife's death while giving birth to their first child had taken its toll. His son, Daniel, had received everything he needed for his well-being except affection. Shuttled from one military school to another, Daniel could never reconcile the colonel to the fact that he had no interest in a military career.

Having inherited his father's stubbornness Daniel had rebelled. A brilliant law student, he built up a highly successful law practice with his best friend, a former college roommate, Charles Brislain.

Specializing in corporate law, their office had grown to seven full-time attorneys with full staff in a luxurious Century City office. His partner had collapsed at hearing of Daniel's death, the shock in many ways harder on him than Brandy.

Raised by her godfather and staff after her parents' deaths, Brandy had received the only tenderness the gruff old man was capable of giving. She adored him from the first, determined to repay at each opportunity for the havoc a young girl thrust in a bachelor home assuredly caused.

Brandy remembered being in awe of Daniel during his

infrequent visits from military school and shyly seeking his attention. She and her smitten girl friends wove endless fantasies with Daniel their hero.

The ten-year age difference kept their relationship more like that of brother and sister, though Brandy was always entranced by his wavy gleaming black hair and gray eyes. Medium height, his slender body was graceful, mind keen, temperament even and gentle as he watched her mature to adulthood.

"Could it only be three weeks now?" she whispered poignantly. "Only twenty-one days ago that the highway patrolman came to the door?" His serious face, hesitant voice, and sympathetic manner had warned her beforehand that he had tragic news to relate.

The shock of hearing her husband and child had been killed was imprinted on her mind. To a stranger it was one more early-morning freeway traffic fatality. They were traveling to Pasadena to see Daniel's father—a routine visit that ended abruptly.

Physically run down with influenza, Brandy had stayed behind in their Marina del Rey condominium. She had been so sick, she couldn't risk kissing her baby good-bye or holding the precious little body in her arms for one last time.

Crying inwardly with the injustice of life, Brandy knew the precarious health of the colonel would benefit by her poise and equanimity during his period of mourning. With strict self-control Brandy was able to retain her own composure while in the presence of others.

The necessities of seeing to a double funeral and aiding her stricken godfather had helped the first week pass. Finding the emptiness of their large home depressing, she

36

came close to giving in to the self-pity expected by her well-meaning friends.

The sight of her daughter's room with its dainty furniture, toys, and tiny frilly dresses painstakingly sewn with loving fingers became too much to bear. For her own mental health she knew she had to leave. Oceanfront condominiums were in constant demand and Charles Brislain had given her a fair price. She knew he had his own reasons for wanting to live there. Escrow was hastened, the deed transferred, and the move completed.

She gave her daughter's things to charity, with the exception of her first baby dress, matching embroidered coat, hat, and shoes. She had spent weeks of anticipation sewing each delicate stitch by hand. Carefully wrapped, they were concealed in the bottom of her cedar chest along with the flop-eared stuffed teddy bear retrieved at the last minute from the charity pickup van. These would be the only permanent reminders of her beloved child.

The colonel's ill health and loneliness prompted the decision to move into his home for a short while. Raised in his lovely old house, she had felt it was like coming home again, although the intervening years had wrought irreparable changes.

Brandy had left as an innocent bride and returned as a grieving widow who had lost her beloved daughter and young husband due to the reckless lane change of a speeding motorist. Her tiny raven-haired little daughter with unique smoke-gray eyes had been the recipient of her abundant love during the last four years of marriage. Her death had inspired the decision to go to Nevada.

"Mrs. Harcourt!" Gracie called out, followed by a discreet knock. "James has settled the colonel in his room and he's demanding you come see him."

"Thank you, Gracie," Brandy answered, opening the door to follow her downstairs. "Could you bring us a drink and some sandwiches? I haven't eaten today, and the colonel will no doubt be starving for a cup of your excellent homemade vegetable soup."

"Of course, Mrs. Harcourt. It will only take me a moment to fix a lunch tray."

At the bottom of the stairs Brandy smiled and, as the housekeeper returned to the kitchen, turned in time to see James exit her godfather's suite.

In his middle sixties James had acted as butler, chauffeur, and valet for twenty years. He had been like an uncle to Brandy and was a devoted employee to her godfather. The two men were good friends and provided companionship to each other, having no relatives or other close friends.

Brandy could tell by the concern on James's face that the colonel was not doing well. Filled with compassion, she placed her hand on his arm.

"How is he, James?"

A slender man of medium height, he bowed his balding head, his blue eyes filled with sadness as he shook his head.

"Not good, Miss Brandy. The death of his son seems to have affected his health drastically. His strength has been precarious, as you know. I—I hope he can bear this double tragedy."

"Did the hospital give you a report?"

"The doctor knew I was concerned and told me he's as fit as any man of eighty-two with angina."

"Well, we'll just have to take extra special care of him, James, won't we?" Brandy spoke with compassion. "Between us and with Gracie's cooking he'll be good as new in a few weeks."

"That isn't so and you know it, but I appreciate your attempt to cheer me up." A deep frown creased his brow as he looked at Brandy's lovely young face, a face of haunting beauty, with deep sadness in her eyes—sadness he had observed many times the last few years but, aware of his position, refused to comment on.

"Is there something else, James?" Brandy asked, knowing she was the only one he could talk to about her godfather now.

"Yes. If you want to know, I think he's grieving that he wasn't more loving to his son. It bears on his mind now that he never showed the boy any affection nor praised him for the success of his law practice."

"But that's so common when one dies, James. Most everyone remembers things he didn't do or say. We can't move the clock back, so we have to be strong enough not to bear in mind those things we regret."

"True, Miss Brandy, but most people don't have your composure. I know your grief is deep, but your concern for others is more important to you than your own pain. Another thing the colonel won't mention is the little girl."

"I know, James. Godfather's devotion to Denise was unquestionable, though we haven't seen him weep."

"That's just it. He's afraid to, for fear you'd break down. Personally I think he misses his granddaughter the most. Her laughter and love touched us all. A void that unfortunately can't be replaced."

Brandy's breath caught at the implication of James's remark. He would be as stunned as her godfather when she was certain she was pregnant. The knowledge that Brandy was carrying a child would be the incentive the colonel needed to snap out of his debilitating depression.

No one in the world would ever know it wasn't Daniel's

child. Brandy would protect the knowledge of her deception with her life if necessary. She never doubted Brad would father a tiny raven-haired child with smoke-gray eyes, a child close enough to Daniel and Denise's coloring to never cause a suspicious glance.

On impulse Brandy placed a kiss on James's leathery cheek before smiling. "Things will work out, James. You wait and see if they don't. In a few weeks we'll all be back to normal."

"You're an angel child, Miss Brandy. You'd make any man believe whatever you'd tell him."

"Thank you, James. I think I should visit the colonel now or he'll take out his anger on you later when you play checkers."

With a graceful turn she left him, walking down the hall to her godfather's door. Her thoughts turned to James's last statement, that her word would be enough. The time might come soon when she would need to convince many people she was telling the truth.

Brandy knocked twice before opening the door. Her eyes were riveted on the frail figure of her godfather, his thick head of gray hair pillowed as he lay in the middle of a large old-fashioned bed. His room was Spartan without knickknacks or a single feminine touch, a holdover from his military days. He detested clutter of any kind, reflected in the other rooms of his house with the exception of Brandy's dainty room and the well-equipped kitchen.

Tears came unbidden to her eyes as she saw the change in his health since the recent tragedy. She rushed to his side and knelt beside the bed, her face laying on his hand before kissing the wrinkled skin and looking into his eyes as they flickered open.

"I'm glad you're home, Godfather. I—I missed you," she told him, tenderness flooding her heart as he gripped her fingers.

"Me too, child. This is where I belong and now where you belong."

"Are you hungry? I had Gracie fix us a tray. You know you shouldn't quit eating because you're temporarily under the weather."

"Grieving for my son and grandchild, you mean, Brandy?"

Brandy rose to sit on the side of his bed, her clear eyes filled with compassion as she answered, "Yes, I mean grieving, but even that has to end. Daniel and Denise wouldn't want us to be sad, would they?"

"No, but life seems so futile now. I—I have nothing to look forward to anymore. I—I was determined to see my grandchild graduate from high school. Why, Brandy . . . ? Tell me why."

"I don't know, Godfather, but I do believe there is a purpose, a reason for everything. You had Daniel for thirty-six years and I—we both had Denise for four. Those were years we might otherwise have had to live without."

A knock interrupted their deep introspection as Gracie waited to be told to enter.

"Come in, Gracie," Brandy called, surreptitiously wiping tears from her face. "I hope you're starving, Godfather, or I'll have to finish the entire tray full of goodies by myself."

The colonel chuckled for the first time since the accident as he glanced over the tray filled with tempting tidbits prepared by his housekeeper.

"You're such a little bit of a thing, Brandy, you won't

have room for much. If you prop up my pillow and fetch a lap tray, I'll join you with a bowl of soup."

Fussing to see that he was comfortable, Brandy served a steaming cup of soup. She buttered a slice of fresh-baked wheat bread and placed it alongside his silverware before sitting at the bedside table.

Brandy was suddenly hungry. Her last meal had been in Las Vegas. Anticipating her evening, she had been too nervous to swallow more than a few bites.

It seemed impossible that she and Brad had shared the most intimate of all contact between two people yet had not shared a simple meal. Two drinks, two hours, and two volatile couplings, and they parted.

How could I? How could I cold-bloodedly seek a man like I did? Her thoughts tormented her, though she knew in the deepest recesses of her heart that her regret was not for what she had done, but that she would never see Brad again. Her mind was filled with thoughts of Brad more often now than those of Daniel. The reasons she dared not face.

Pleased that the colonel was sipping his soup, she picked up a sandwich, hoping he wouldn't notice her contemplative mood.

"Hmm, my favorite." She glanced at her godfather, biting into the bacon, tomato, and avocado sandwich. "Creamy smooth avocado makes a plain sandwich fit for a king."

"You've certainly changed, child. You used to think they were terrible," he reminded her, smiling as she reached for another half sandwich.

"They're delicious now. I've changed tastes in many things lately."

"Did you get everything settled with Brislain?" he asked, changing the subject abruptly.

"Yes. Escrow is completed. The money is deposited in the bank and I'm free of all responsibility now. He bought the furniture too. I only needed to move my personal things."

"Good. I could never understand why Daniel insisted on living way down there anyway. This house could hold a half-dozen families."

"You know why, Godfather. It's not right for a newly married couple to live with—with someone else. They—they need to be . . . alone." *My God, what a hypocrite I am,* she thought, refusing to think about her and Daniel's relationship.

Brandy noticed the colonel give a weary sigh before motioning to her to remove the tray from his lap. Seeing to his comfort, Brandy placed a kiss on his cheek before gathering their lunch things together and tiptoeing from the room. A final glimpse showed he was already starting to fall asleep.

She walked to the kitchen, placing the tray with most of the food untouched on the sink counter. Thanking Gracie, she walked to her room. Inside, with the door locked, she relaxed, her body weary from tension and lack of sleep. Unused to sleeping in the daytime she felt foolish to be undressing so early in the day. Nevertheless she put on her favorite gold silk pajamas with the mandarin collar and frog fastenings and slipped between cool percale sheets.

A flush touched her face as she realized the last time she had been to bed. She turned on her side and drew her legs up, arms hugged across her abdomen. Pain knifed through her, knowing she would never see Brad again.

"Oh, Lord, what have I done? I can't get him out of my mind," she moaned, tears slipping unbidden from beneath her clenched eyelids.

It was impossible for her to forget the trauma of his lovemaking. His consideration for her pleasure before, during, and in the aftermath of sex was unbelievable. He couldn't have been more tender or reverent if he had been in love with her.

Brad's hard male form, possessive touch, and virile nature had left her fulfilled. His awakening had shown her the beauty of sexual pleasures between man and woman. She knew her desire to repeat the experience with Brad would cause her unlimited distress. Her chaste bed already seemed barren. After one brief affair she yearned to be cradled in the strength of his steel-hard arms.

With thoughts of Brad filling her mind Brandy drifted into a deep sleep. Exhausted by the need for composure and endless nights of insomnia, she didn't awaken until late the following morning.

CHAPTER THREE

For three weeks Brandy stayed close to her godfather's side, attentive to his every need. Her heart was saddened when it appeared the old man was growing more apathetic. His iron will and self-determination seemed to have deserted him with the loss of his son and granddaughter.

An avid gardener, he had spent hours in faded coveralls, helping the landscaper keep the colorful flower beds surrounding the house in healthy splendor. His vivid green lawns, aged trees, and array of blossoms were the envy of the neighborhood. His leathery tanned hands and face now began to pale as he refused to venture outside.

Gracie's excellent cooking failed to tempt his waning appetite, his weight loss visible in the fit of his clothes. Aware that his heart couldn't stand the stress of continued grief, Brandy called his local doctor for the third time that week.

She paced the living room as she waited for him to complete his examination. Footsteps on the polished oak floors warned her prior to his appearance.

Without preamble she questioned, "How is he, Doctor Epstein?"

The family doctor from even before Brandy had arrived, he had watched her mature, attended her wedding and the funeral of her husband and child. He admired her straightforward manner and composure all through her grief; he knew it would be foolish to deceive her about her godfather's precarious health.

"He's deteriorating quickly, my dear." Taking her hand, he watched as tears spilled from the corners of her expressive amber eyes. Filled with compassion for her sudden misfortune and the burdens resting solely on her narrow shoulders, he offered his sympathy.

"I'm sorry, Brandy. He's an old friend, but that's his main problem now. His age is against his recovery if he doesn't snap out of his despondency."

Brandy wiped the tears from her cheeks with the back of her hands, shaking her head in understanding.

"I've tried everything, Doctor, but he won't respond." Wringing her hands, she walked to the fireplace, her eyes caught by the large oil painting over the mantel. It showed the colonel in his youth wearing full-dress uniform, his shoulders squared, piercing eyes a steely blue. It was hard to believe it was the same person as the frail old man lying listlessly in his bedroom.

"Is there anything at all you could suggest, Doctor? I thought my moving in with him for a few months might help, but it hasn't appeared to."

James appeared from the foyer carrying the doctor's overcoat. Dr. Epstein took it before looking at the two concerned faces.

"I think a change would do him good. A change of location actually. If you and James could take him away for a few days, it might help. Somewhere warmer possibly. We've had an unusual amount of rainy weather lately."

"I've suggested that, Doctor, but he adamantly refuses

to leave his home. I'll see what I can do though. Maybe a different approach would work."

A sudden decision came to Brandy. She would not wait for a positive pregnancy check. Certain in her own mind that she was going to have a child, she could hardly wait to tell her godfather. A little psychology on her part should do the trick.

"Thank you, Doctor Epstein. I feel confident I won't have to phone your office for the rest of the year."

"My child, I certainly think you have an idea forming. Remember to send me a postcard if you leave." Nodding to James, he left the house, encouraged by the sudden look of excitement on Brandy's face. If anyone could help his old friend, Brandy could. Her youth and exuberance for life would be a powerful stimulant to anyone.

Brandy looked at James's face, his depression nearly as bad as her godfather's. *The entire household is gloomy,* Brandy thought, dismayed by the way they all tiptoed around in silence, fearful lest a smile or touch of humor would show that they didn't commiserate with the recent trauma.

She took James's arm, smiling at his startled face.

"Come with me, James. I would like you to be with me when I tell the colonel the news. I think it will make you both equally happy."

They walked to her godfather's room and entered after a brief knock.

James stood back, hands clasped before him as he waited for Brandy to greet his employer.

After rushing across the room, Brandy knelt beside the colonel's bed, her usual habit since the accident. She kissed his hand, placing her cheek against it affectionately before looking up at his lined face.

"Hello, my child," he whispered. "Did the doctor tell you I wouldn't be around much longer?"

"No, he did not. He did imply you were a stubborn old man who needs to take a vacation," she quipped, trying to humor him before she gave him her news.

"Stubborn old man." Noticing the twinkle in Brandy's eyes, he settled down after his brief outburst. "Now tell me the truth, Brandy. What did he say?"

"He said you need a change. A short trip would do us all good, he felt."

Shaking his head in disagreement, he looked at James standing quietly just inside the door. "Come in, James. I suppose you are conspiring with the two of them to get me to leave my home?"

"No, sir, but I do think it might be a good idea. The Cadillac could use the trip if nothing else. If you don't start letting me chauffeur you somewhere, we'll have to replace the battery."

A sudden look of pain crossed his face before he told them in a dejected tone, "I don't care anymore, James. It's just an old car that, like me, has outgrown its usefulness."

"No, Godfather. That's not true," Brandy cried out.

"Yes . . . yes, it is. I have nothing to live for now. Don't think I haven't noticed how you've changed too, child. You were always such a ray of sunshine in my life, now you're withering away. If you lose anymore weight, you'll blow afield."

"Don't be silly, Godfather. I'm strong as a horse," she retorted quickly, trying to bring a smile to his face.

"Never a horse. You're too tiny to compare with anything that big."

Squeezing his hand, she rose to sit on the edge of the

bed. "Come here, James, please," she said quietly. "I want you both to hear my news."

Fatigue crossed the colonel's face as he leaned against the pillow, his eyes watching his goddaughter's face apathetically.

"What news, Brandy?" he asked before crossing his hands across his chest listlessly.

"Well, Godfather, what would you think if I told you that I was—"

The colonel's hand wavered, dismissing them rudely, his eyes closing. "I don't want to hear anything else today."

"Not even the news that I'm going to have a child?" she asked, her voice filled with soft affection as she watched for his reaction.

His eyes opened, his face transformed before her eyes at the news. Tears ran down his cheeks as he opened his arms to her.

"Oh, my child, my precious Brandy! Are you certain?"

"Yes, Godfather. I'm pregnant."

"When did the doctor confirm it?"

A rosy flush tinged her face before her lashes lowered to shield the sudden feeling of remorse over her hypocrisy.

"I don't need a doctor yet. A woman who's had a child . . . knows when she is pregnant . . . again."

Sitting up in bed, he took her hand. "That's why you've lost weight, isn't it? You've had morning sickness and didn't even let us know." His hands were misshapen with arthritis, the knuckles swollen and painful, but his grip was as firm as a young man's at the news he would be a grandfather again.

Tears filled Brandy's eyes at the happiness expressed by the colonel. The traumatic events that led to her conviction that she was pregnant were made worthwhile. *Forgive me, Brad,* she cried inwardly. *I used you so terribly, but my need was strong.* She was certain that he had forgotten her, but if not, she would undoubtedly be only a fleeting memory. An immoral young woman intent on having her first affair. Her thoughts were interrupted by her godfather's voice.

"James . . . get to the kitchen and have Gracie fix this child a high-protein meal. Furthermore you watch that she finishes it all."

"But, Godfather . . . you'll have me fat as a pig."

"Get out of here. Both of you. I need my rest if I'm going to put up with diapers and baby bottles around the house."

"Not for several months yet," Brandy reminded him. "I'm certain I became pregnant right before—before Daniel died."

The colonel watched Brandy's face, his thoughts now devoted to her well-being. "James." His eyes filled with tears of delight before demanding abruptly, "Make arrangements for the three of us to travel to Phoenix. This child needs to relax in the sun." As if it were his own idea to get a change of scenery, he told James to make plans to leave by the coming weekend.

"Thank you, Godfather." Brandy smiled, hugging him before standing at the foot of his bed. "I'd like that. It'll be nice to get a tan before I get too awkward to lay around in a bikini."

Leaving after James, Brandy walked to the kitchen. With a shock she realized she was suddenly starving. She touched her stomach, the image of Brad's child flooding her mind.

The colonel's health was still worrisome to Brandy, but

his interest in her welfare preceded his own frailty. They spent hours each day looking at travel brochures, trying to decide where they wanted to stay. They had still not made up their mind the following Thursday when James brought them the mail.

As her godfather watched, Brandy sorted the letters. A long beige envelope in heavy stationery with brown printing, addressed to the colonel, caught her eye. It was from the Casa del Oro resort in Palm Springs. She looked it over curiously.

"Did you request information from Palm Springs as well as Phoenix?"

"No. Better open it and see what it is. Probably an advertisement to throw away," he answered without interest.

Brandy carefully slit the envelope, taking the sheets of paper and reading them out loud to her godfather.

"But I don't understand. You've won a three-week stay for you and your guests effective immediately." She raised her eyes, the letter open in her lap, and looked at the colonel.

"Do you know anything about this?"

"No. It's probably a sales gimmick. Why don't you phone them and tell them we're not interested," he told her bluntly.

"I'll check, but this is not a form letter. I've heard they have the reputation of being one of the most outstanding resorts in town. This could be the answer to our plans. But I can't understand why you would get invited. You haven't been to Palm Springs for several years now."

"Don't procrastinate. Get on the phone. I don't care how or why. If this is authentic, we'll leave tomorrow."

Brandy walked to the library to phone, her fingers

drumming nervously on the desktop as she listened to the phone ring. Within minutes she had confirmed that her godfather indeed had a free three-week vacation reserved. There were no strings attached to the offer, and the manager seemed insulted that she should think it was a sales gimic. She was told that Casa del Oro was not now nor in the past and foreseeable future offering shares for sale to the public.

Amused by his affronted voice, Brandy made reservations for the next afternoon. She called James, telling him to pack his and the colonel's things, as they would all be leaving at ten o'clock the next morning.

She told her godfather the news, then walked to her room. Going through her wardrobe, crammed with the latest fashions, she debated the rest of the afternoon on what and what not to take.

The following day she stepped into the backseat of the Cadillac, sitting beside her godfather. The trunk was filled with their suitcases before James got into the driver's seat, his dark uniform and cap giving him an arrogant air equal to the colonel's.

Brandy smiled at the two old men as they eased out of the driveway. She would have preferred to follow them in her Porsche, but her wishes were vehemently overruled. Pleased at their concern, she agreed, planning to rent a car so she could explore the area and let the two men entertain themselves in their own way.

James competently maneuvered the gleaming Cadillac from the tree-shaded road that fronted her godfather's home and onto Orange Grove Avenue before traveling north toward Pasadena's main street, Colorado Boulevard.

Brandy laid down the brochures on Palm Springs that

she had been reading and glanced disinterestedly out the side window, noticing the crowds strolling around Norton Simon's Museum of Art. She had spent many hours browsing through the unique structure, admiring priceless paintings dating from the fifteenth century, tapestries, and sculptures. Always interested in art, she had stared in awe at works by Rubens, Picasso, Van Gogh, Rembrandt, El Greco, and Matisse.

As James pulled onto the eastbound 210 Foothill Freeway, it brought back memories of the world-renowned New Year's Day Rose Parade and the ensuing crowd of sightseer's that jammed Pasadena's sidewalks, vying for a curb-side seat. Arriving from many countries and most states, people viewed the famed parade before many continued on to watch the annual Rose Bowl football game.

Brandy's thoughts were interrupted by the colonel giving James directions. He unnecessarily reminded him to turn southeast when they got to San Bernardino and then take Interstate Highway 10.

"Godfather, you're hopeless," Brandy sighed lovingly. "James has driven the local freeways chauffeuring you around for twenty years. I doubt very much if he would make a wrong turn today." Brandy smiled as her eyes caught James's resigned look in the rearview mirror. He was used to his employer's constant comments and chiding.

Pleased to be leaving the unusually damp weather hanging over the San Gabriel Valley and the greater Los Angeles basin, the colonel abruptly ordered James to stop at the first restaurant near Redlands. "Pull off soon, James. I want my bowl of soup and Brandy needs to eat. Feeding two now, you know. I don't want my last grandchild to be scrawny and undernourished." Tears brimmed the colonel's eyes as he thought of Daniel. "I never did under-stand my son, Brandy," he spoke honestly, his voice trem-bling with sadness. He glanced at his goddaughter before briefly clasping her hand in a tight grip. "I have a feeling you'll bear me a robust grandson who will be a proud Marine."

Brandy placed her soft hand sympathetically on her godfather's knee, giving him a tender smile. "I think you might be right, Godfather. If I have a boy this time, I wouldn't be at all surprised if he competed with his grand-father's heroics." Suddenly turning her head sideways, she looked out the window, her sight blurred by tears.

Brad's image filled her mind, followed by the sudden vision of him holding on to the small trusting hand of a young child. A handsome boy with sturdy shoulders, tousled black hair, and haunting gray eyes.

Oh, God, what have I done? Brandy's cry was silent. Deep in thought over her deception, she was filled with remorse. *How could I have deliberately planned to get pregnant, only to deny the father a rightful place in his child's life?*

As James pulled to a smooth stop she felt her godfa-ther's hand touch her shoulder, his voice suddenly show-ing his former strength. "Don't torment your mind with what cannot be replaced, child," he told her, mistaking her silence for grief over Daniel and Denise.

Good advice but hard—no, impossible—to heed, she thought before giving her godfather and James a radiant smile. "Let's eat lunch now, you two." Opening the car door before James could assist the colonel from the back-seat, she called over her shoulder, "Last one inside pays the bill."

Later Brandy watched as her godfather finished the last

spoonful of his soup. She had listened without surprise as he complained throughout their meal that the chef didn't know how to make eatable soup.

"Probably came from a package or a can. Right, James?"

Brandy's laughter was light as she laid a tip on the table for the exasperated waitress. "All the crackers you crumble into your soup, Godfather, I'm surprised you can even tell what kind it is," she teased as they rose to leave.

The freeway undulated as it curved east through the small rural towns of Beaumont and Banning. Coming to Highway 111, James turned right for the final eleven miles to the fashionable desert playground of America's most distinguished personalities, from U.S. presidents to top figures in entertainment, sports, and business.

Brandy thumbed through the travel brochure again, reading about the resort. Originally founded as a sanitorium in the early 1900s, Palm Springs, located in the upper Colorado Desert beneath the precipitous slopes of the San Jacinto Peak, nearly eleven thousand feet high, now has year-round popularity although its warm dry climate brought it fame as a winter resort. Brandy had heard about the mineral springs in the city, reputed to have great healing powers. Created in 1000 B.C. when huge tremors caused the San Andreas Fault, the natural crystal-clear waters still flowed. Brandy hoped that for her godfather's sake the legend was true. The brochure explained that the springs were discovered by the Agua Caliente band of Cahuilla Indians, who were the first settlers in the area and who had lived in the canyon for centuries.

She lifted her gaze and looked through the window at the scenery, imagining how it had changed. The isolation of the canyon and the sands disappeared as they reached the city proper and surrounding hillsides where luxurious homes abounded.

Brandy watched curiously as well-dressed men and women, most with deep tans, browsed along Palm Canyon Drive, the main thoroughfare. Their colorful resort clothes proved that shopping was a popular diversion. Broad concrete sidewalks fronted pace-setting boutiques, franchised eating places, privately owned restaurants, and department stores with cleverly designed window displays. Lighted palm trees served as streetlamps. Brandy imagined it must be a unique sight at night.

The heavy influx of sun worshipers and golfers appeared to be enjoying the peak winter season. Known as the Winter Golf Capital, Palm Springs hosts world-famous tournaments on some of its many courses. Turning southeast of town, James slowed down, preparing to change lanes.

A low adobe fence formed a graceful boundary around the acres of lush dark green lawn. Casa del Oro beckoned, a veritable oasis in the desert. Massive wrought-iron lamps hung in ornate splendor on each side of the heavy carved timber entrance sign. Exotic palm trees towered over the curved drive leading to the luxurious three-story whitewashed resort. Each room had its own iron balcony. The wide roof and enclosed walkways were covered with overlapping curved tiles of dull red clay. Its overall picture emerged welcoming and peaceful in the bright afternoon sunlight.

Brandy suddenly looked forward to the weeks ahead. She longed to sight-see and had always reveled in the warmth of a clear desert atmosphere. The three-hour drive to Palm Springs had made her restless, Brad's image relentlessly tormenting her mind. Her nerves were taut and she needed time alone to unwind and regain her wavering composure.

This tranquil beauty is what we all need, Brandy reflected. Impressed by the courtesy of the parking attendant, she and the colonel entered the air-conditioned foyer. The sudden change in temperature was a startling contrast from the unseasonably warm March day.

She glanced around appreciatively. Expecting Casa del Oro to be plush, she was stunned by its tasteful beauty. Polished imported tile flooring, dark Spanish furnishings, and the dense profusion of potted plants reaching toward the beamed ceiling were aesthetically appealing.

Brandy seated her godfather in a comfortable chair before going to the elaborately carved reception counter. The effusive welcome, when she identified herself, took her by surprise. The manager's eyes were frankly appraising as he introduced himself and welcomed her and the colonel to the resort. He motioned to a waiting assistant, who stepped forward to take them to their suite. Entering a vast living area, she scanned the affluent decor quickly. A corner wet bar, broad cushioned sofas, deep armchairs, large screen color TV, and writing desk holding a basket filled with a variety of choice fruits showed thoughtful policy.

She turned as James came in, followed by a uniformed attendant with their luggage. Setting some of the cases down, the young man spoke to Brandy. "If you will follow me, Mrs. Harcourt, I will take you to your room now. This lower suite contains only two bedrooms. One for Colonel Harcourt and one for his valet."

The attendant escorted her on the elevator to the top floor and to the end of the north wing into another luxurious suite. From the first moment she passed through the carved wood door and glanced around the interior, she loved it. Her breath caught at the beauty and unexpected privacy of having her own spacious sitting room-bedroom combination.

Her feet sank into the deep-piled earth-colored carpeting. A king-size bed was covered with an intricate tapestry spread matching long drapes pulled to each side of glass patio doors. Rugged mountains were visible in the distance across the south wing. Her own basket of succulent fruit sat atop a glass-topped wrought-iron table surrounded by amber chairs. Heady bouquets of red roses filled several vases. Opening the louver doors to the right, she was shocked to see a lounging area and an immense sunken pool.

"Oh, my gosh!" Brandy exclaimed, laughter bubbling from her throat as she looked at the sensual room. "This surely can't be for me. I think there has been some mistake."

The young man eyed her lovely face boldly before shaking his head no. "Our reservation supervisor's explanation was emphatic that this is to be your suite indefinitely."

"Well, I don't expect to be here that long," Brandy chuckled as she walked forward to explore the third room, a separate dressing room and bath. Returning, she gazed at the sunken pool quizzically.

"That's a hot pool with whirl-jet hydra-massage. It's very relaxing after an afternoon of tennis or horseback riding."

"Casa del Oro has that too?" Brandy asked, walking into the suite.

"Yes, along with golf, racquetball, shuffleboard, badminton, bridge tournaments, sauna baths, bicycle trails, and gyms."

"Boredom should never be a problem, then," she responded before restlessly walking onto the broad balcony overlooking a central courtyard. It was almost like living in one's own special world, she thought, looking with pleasure at the shimmering blue water of an Olympic-size swimming pool. It was crowded with the cavorting bodies of men and women, as was the smaller circular pool filled with mineral water.

Brandy thanked the young man politely and reached to hand him a tip.

He refused courteously, then explained that dinner was served in the Fireside Room from five o'clock until eleven. "We offer a variety of magnificent cuisine from gourmet dining to hearty meals or quick snacks in our coffee shop, which is open twenty-four hours. Our bar opens at noon, with the best combo in town playing five nights a week."

"This sounds more like paradise all the time," she exclaimed before closing the door, puzzled by her godfather's free accommodations.

Brandy unpacked her clothes, took a relaxing bath in the regular bathtub, then slipped into an amber silk lounging gown before relaxing on the bed.

Thoughts of Brad tormented her as she lay her head on the wide pillows against the headboard. It was the same size bed they had lain on in the aftermath of passion. The memory of their affair refused to dim with time. It had been four weeks, yet she could close her eyes and feel his touch as if he were in the room. The scent of his aftershave, the abrasive sensuality of his hair-roughened chest rubbing her naked breasts, and the warmth of his hands caressing her back were each lucid memories.

She touched her stomach. She was more than two weeks overdue and totally certain she was going to bear Brad's baby in eight months time. Eight long months before she could hold his child to her breast. Tears slipped from her eyes as she thought of her darling Denise. Deep sobs were torn from her throat as she flung herself facedown on the bed, crying for the first time since the afternoon she returned from Las Vegas. Before long she fell into a restless sleep.

CHAPTER FOUR

The shrill ring of the bedside phone unexpectedly awakened her, startling her out of sleep. Her godfather's voice, sounding more confident than it had in weeks, invited her to join him and James in the lounge for a before-dinner drink.

She declined, agreeing to meet him in the dining room instead. With care Brandy applied makeup, then brushed her hair until it lay in gleaming waves across her shoulders, feathered around her face. The excellent cut enhanced its natural curl.

Clad in beige lace briefs and plunging bra, she reached for a long-sleeve silk blouse in deep rust. A full-length skirt of rust velvet with inserts of gold and brown print running vertically gave her added height.

She fastened several gold chains of alternating lengths around her neck before slipping on high-heeled sandals. A subtle spray of perfume, and she was ready.

Her vivid hair, petite figure, and exquisite face drew all eyes as she approached the dining room. It was crowded with well-dressed people. Deep booths lined the walls, their high curved backs separating the tables with complete privacy. She followed the maître d'hôtel through the darkened room, impressed that all the employees wore black slacks, ruffled white shirts, and boleros above gold cummerbunds. Very chic.

Her godfather sat alone at a table for three. His eyes were bright with admiration as he looked at Brandy. His long rest and sudden interest in life had given him renewed vigor.

"Sit down, Brandy. You look lovely, my child."

Brandy leaned down to kiss his cheek before asking, "Where's James?"

"You know he never dines with us at night."

"But the table is set for three. I thought he had finally agreed to join us for dinner."

"We're having dinner with the owner. He was called away for a moment but will return. We are to look at the menu and choose anything we wish. I hadn't realized the meals were included with our vacation."

Brandy picked up the large menu, contemplating what to order. She felt distracted and paid little attention as the colonel extolled the virtues of their host. It was obvious that he and her godfather had shared confidences over their predinner cocktails.

"I think I'll have jumbo prawns, Godfather."

"Excellent idea, Mrs. . . . . er—Harcourt," a man standing alongside her agreed casually, his husky voice interrupting their conversation. "We serve excellent seafood broiled over mesquite wood. Prawns skewered on wooden picks with bacon and dipped in drawn butter have an unforgettable flavor."

As she turned, Brandy's face paled. It was Brad! Her hands trembled as he took the menu from her before easing his hips into the seat on her right. She swallowed convulsively, too stunned by his unexpected appearance to utter a sound. Head bowed, she waited, refusing to look

62

up. With her dark lashes tightly closed she prayed for strength to face him.

She had never believed there was the remotest possibility they would meet again. To come face to face so unexpectedly brought back the memories of their shared passion with startling clarity. Pain pierced her breast as she fought for composure.

"Would you introduce us, Colonel? Your daughter-in-law appears to be . . . shy."

Brandy flinched when she felt Brad's leg move next to hers so that their thighs were touching. She could feel the power of his eyes, knew he was staring at her face. Unable to stand the torment, she slowly raised her heavy lashes as her godfather introduced her.

"Brandy, this is Brad Lucas. Owner of Casa del Oro and an ex-Marine captain. He has been gracious enough to extend me his personal welcome."

Her eyes raised, their deep amber color darkening with fear as she looked at Brad for the first time. She was aware that one false word of her indiscretion could endanger her godfather's precarious health, so she silently beseeched him to remain mute. His expression was enigmatic, eyes narrowed as he returned her look. The tenderness she remembered so vividly had turned to cool steely gray. The colonel looked on, unaware of the turmoil churning in her or the tensions between them.

Brad's smile was grim as he spoke. "I would like to offer you my hospitality also, Mrs. Harcourt. May I call you Brandy, please? Somehow Mrs. Harcourt sounds wrong, if you'll pardon me saying so, Colonel."

He reached forward, touching Brandy's hand, deliberately pressing into the platinum band of her wedding ring until she drew away in pain, nodding her head in answer to his question.

"Everything . . . everything I have is yours, Brandy. You'll find my resort well equipped. Both for outdoor and *indoor* pleasures."

In instant rapport with Brad the colonel wanted his entire regard. He leaned forward, his voice cutting the mounting tension. "I was telling Brandy how gracious you are, Brad, to extend us this gratuitous vacation. We were actually preparing to travel to Phoenix when your offer arrived. This is much more to my liking, as I didn't want to travel too far from home. You appear to have a magnificent desert resort. One to make any man proud."

Her godfather's enthusiasm and liking for Brad were obvious. The colonel rarely called anyone by their first name. Brandy could not remember him ever doing so with anyone on first acquaintance. Brad's vigorous strength and youth seemed to remove the last of the colonel's depression. The old man's eyes sparkled as he watched them both covertly.

Brandy sat in silence, mind whirling with trepidation as she waited for Brad to speak. Her hands were clenched nervously in her lap as she prayed he would keep silent about their meeting in Nevada.

"Thank you, Colonel. Casa del Oro rooms have been compared with those in . . . Las Vegas. We have only king-size beds. No doubt due to my size."

Brad's left hand reached surreptitiously under the table to grip Brandy's trembling fingers. The hold was firm, his warmth searing her skin as she remembered the details of their previous intimacy and her uninhibited response. The subtle innuendo of his words brought a flush to her face.

"Now, you, Brandy, are so petite, you might risk getting lost altogether in our beds."

"Hardly!" she retorted, wanting the intimate conversation to end immediately.

"Well, you must admit you are small enough to almost fit in a man's pocket." Unabashed by her spurt of temper and indrawn breath, Brad pinned her gaze before asking, "Would you like a drink before we order? Our bartender mixes excellent screwdrivers—unless that is too potent for a lady."

Her eyes flashed sparks, warning him she would not be browbeaten despite his having the upper hand at the moment. She received a momentary feeling of pleasure at his flinch, knowing the sharp kick aimed at his shin had connected. They would have to have a confrontation. It was inevitable that she seek his compassion in not relating anything of their past to her godfather.

"Well, Brandy?" the colonel interrupted her thoughts. "Do you want a drink or not? If not, then let's order. It's been a long time since lunch."

Her eyes left the taut planes of Brad's handsome face to glance at her godfather. The tone of her voice softened as she smiled affectionately. "I don't want anything"—a brief glance back to Brad—"but a quiet dinner."

Brad motioned to the hovering waiter and placed their dinner requests with casual ease.

To cover the nervousness building up within her from the continued pressure of his muscular thigh, plus the blatant caress of his fingers against her knee while ordering their meal, Brandy blurted out, "Your—your waiters look extremely chic. I like their outfits, Mr. . . ."

"Lucas. An easy name to remember, I've been told, though I insist you call me Brad. I feel as if you are an *intimate* friend already. And the colonel too of course," he added, smiling.

Brandy refused to take the bait of his comments as she continued, "I was going to say, Mr. Lucas, that—"

"Brad!"

"Very well. Brad. I was going to commend their outfits. They complement the Spanish decor."

"Thank you. As you may have noticed, most of my staff is male. Many women alone stay here. Spinsters, divorcées, some even . . . married . . . or widowed. Without fail they all enjoy having good-looking young men wait on them." With added emphasis he questioned, "If you ever traveled alone, wouldn't you find the trip more to your liking with the devoted attentiveness of one—or more—men?"

"No!"

The colonel looked up from his bowl of soup to comment, his tone gruff as he reminded Brad, "Apparently you forgot that Brandy is still grieving for my son. She's only been widowed seven weeks now." He reached out to touch Brandy's hand, squeezing her fingers, thinking her pale face was due to thoughts of Daniel. "She never looked at another man but Daniel. Not many women in this world faithful to one man anymore, is there, Brad?"

"Actually I don't believe I've met a single woman whom I would trust . . . out of my sight. Even the most virtuous often have a scheme when they seek a man's company."

The colonel chuckled slyly. "Sounds like you're a cynic, son. Don't mind if I call you that, do you? You're what I expected Daniel to be. Stubborn boy. Absolutely refused to join the military."

"I'd be flattered if you called me son, Colonel, but don't

you think your son might have felt intimidated by your formidable record in the Marines? It would be pretty hard to live up to."

"Never thought of it that way." His eyes filled with tears as he looked without shame at Brad. "It's too late now to make amends to Daniel. Take my advice, son. If you see anything you want, don't hesitate to seek it. If you have anything in your heart that needs saying, don't hold back. Sometimes it's too late to let our loved ones know how we feel."

Brandy refused to glance at Brad, but his words echoed throughout her mind as she listened to each husky statement.

"I intend to not only seek what I want, Colonel, I plan to get it. Since I've never been one to hold back my thoughts, it goes without saying that I'll voice my desires."

"That's the Marine in you speaking, Brad," the colonel said, laughing, his lined face crinkling as he smiled. His short-clipped gray hair bristled as he bent to slice a juicy bite of filet mignon.

"You aren't eating your prawns, Brandy. Don't you like them?" Brad asked softly, his eyes lingering on her face.

Intent on their conversation, Brandy had let her plate sit before her untouched. Fresh sautéed zucchini, colorful rice pilaf, and jumbo prawns wafted a tantalizing odor, but Brandy knew they would be tasteless. Determined to rebuke Brad, she removed a prawn from the skewer and dipped it in the drawn butter. Her eyes glittered as she stared at him defiantly, her chin raised with stubbornness.

She took the end of the prawn in her mouth, bit off a succulent bit, and chewed it slowly. She was surprised to find it delicious. *Obviously,* she thought, *everything he has anything to do with I seem to enjoy. His lovemaking, his resort, and now his restaurant.*

"Actually I find them quite excellent, Mr. Lucas." She picked up her fork to taste the rice when she felt a sharp pinch on her waist, unobserved by her godfather as he ate his meal.

"Brad!" he scolded. "Use my first name, Brandy."

"Call him Brad, child. We'll be here for three weeks and there's no need to be formal. Brad tells me he plans on showing us around the area during our visit. Has plans for each day in fact."

"What?" Brandy blurted out, choking on her food.

"Let me help you." Brad raised his hand, rubbing it across her back, his touch a caress more than an attempt to ease her discomfort. "I knew a lady once who coughed that same way when she attempted to smoke. In fact, Colonel, your daughter-in-law and she are exactly alike in many ways."

"How?" the colonel asked, his curiosity aroused by Brad's remark. Brandy was so special to him, he couldn't believe that she could be compared with anyone else.

"The innocence, I think. Brandy looks virginal. I find it impossible to believe she was married."

Brandy's breath caught, all color leaving her face.

"Forgive my social blunder, Brandy," he added huskily. "I do not intend for my bluntness to cause you pain."

Without raising her face, Brandy accepted the apology, praying the meal would soon come to an end.

"Good, Brad. This is the sweetest child in the world. I don't think there is a thing she wouldn't do for my happiness."

"Hush, Godfather," Brandy scolded, not wanting him to say any more.

Brad refused to stop his questioning. Stunned by what he had learned so far, he knew he wouldn't rest until he unearthed the entire story of Brandy's unique life. She had haunted him since their brief interlude in Las Vegas. To find out she had been married was unbelievable. There was no doubt in his mind that he had taken her virginity that night. It was impossible that any man with the legal right to do so had not bedded her the moment they were wed.

"You are very lucky, Colonel, to have such a devoted daughter-in-law. Did I hear her call you godfather too?"

"Yes, Brad. I've been doubly blessed. I raised Brandy after her parents' death when she was only seven years old. One of the happiest moments of my life was when she married my son."

"I can understand that," Brad added huskily, his eyes lingering on Brandy's lovely face as she finished drinking a glass of iced tea. "How long were you married, Brandy?"

"Five—five years," she answered softly, placing the glass in its saucer. She leaned back to stare at Brad.

Unperturbed by the warning flashing in her eyes, he continued the interrogation. "Five years! That seems impossible. You must have been very young. Around twenty-one, I'd guess."

"Correct," the colonel told him. "Though most people think she looks younger than twenty-six now. You're very perceptive, Brad. It must be because of your military training."

"Er—yes, possibly," Brad murmured, his eyes refusing to look away from Brandy's face. Aware of the soft flush tinging her cheeks his voice mocked. "Too bad there weren't any children in your marriage."

"Oh, but there was!" the colonel blurted out proudly.

"There was?" Brad questioned abruptly, amazement

barely hidden as he received the most astonishing news yet.

"Yes, they had the most beautiful little girl in the world. She was the image of my son." His voice cracked, tears coming to his eyes at the thought that he would never see them again.

"Godfather, please . . ." Brandy's eyes filled with tears as she pleaded, "Don't talk about it tonight."

Brad was shocked, his mind in a turmoil over the colonel's staggering testimony. He turned toward Brandy, observing her imploring expression when she raised her face to meet his narrow stare. Eyes the color of rich amber fearfully communicated a poignant plea for him to remain silent.

What the hell's going on? His thoughts were puzzled as he wondered, *How could the keen old man possibly believe his goddaughter had given birth to his son's child?*

Aware of Brad's quandary, Brandy immediately lowered her face, hoping to shield her thoughts from his probing glance beneath the thickness of her lashes. *Oh, Lord! How he must hate me now.*

Brad stayed quiet despite his burning anger over her deception. His heart had been touched by her quick indrawn breath when the colonel mentioned the death of her little girl, and he felt her petite body tremble against his side. He clenched his hand, holding her cold shaking fingers until they absorbed the warmth of his palm. Her distress was obvious, yet she had still defied him, retaliating with a brief flare of pride and temper when he taunted her with reminders of their previous intimacy.

Damn the unforgettable little witch! Her naive look belies the memory of her passionate response to my lovemaking in Las Vegas. My God, what other surprises will be in store for me? he pondered angrily. *A married woman for five years, mother of a young daughter, but she comes to me as virtuous and innocent to a man's needs as an infant . . . pleading that I seduce her!*

Brad knew her marriage had been platonic and the child could not be hers by birth. The rest of her mysterious behavior he would demand she clarify later. If she proved uncooperative, he wouldn't hesitate to unravel her story through discreet questioning of the colonel or his valet.

From the corner of his eye Brad spotted his waiter bringing their dessert. Releasing Brandy's hand, he smiled at the colonel. He was intrigued by the old man, liking him instantly, despite his blunt, outspoken, contrary manner. It was immediately apparent how much Brandy cared. Each time she looked at her godfather her expressive face changed to one of tender affection, her eloquent voice becoming soft with love and concern.

Damn him! I hope he knows how lucky he is, Brad thought jealously.

A cart was wheeled to their table, filled with rich pastries, éclairs, elaborate cakes and pies topped with swirls of whipped cream. Brandy, normally having an insatiable sweet tooth, looked on without interest. It was impossible to sit and talk with Brad as if he were a stranger any longer. She had to leave the table or break down completely.

"Would you like dessert?" Brad asked them, refusing any himself.

"No," she answered, looking at the colonel as he pointed to a piece of German chocolate pie. "Godfather . . . could you excuse me, please. I'm so weary and beginning to get a dreadful headache."

Anxious to taste the rich pie, forbidden by his doctors

for several years, he motioned her to leave. "I'll sit here and talk to Brad. We military men talk about things women wouldn't understand anyway. Right, son?"

Brad's eyes searched Brandy's face, alarmed by her sudden loss of color and the pain in her eyes. He stood up to let her slide from the booth, answering the colonel offhandedly, "I don't think our military women would approve of your chauvinism, sir."

As Brandy slipped by him he took her arm, his voice filled with concern. "Will you be all right, Brandy?"

"Yes . . . yes, I'll be fine." His sudden solicitude was her undoing, the hand on her forearm reminding her of the comfort she found within his hold. She glanced upward, her expression poignant as she whispered, "Thank you for the excellent meal, Brad."

She turned toward her godfather and bent to place a kiss on his forehead as he reached to take another bite of pie. "Good night, Godfather. You're not supposed to have rich sweets, you know."

"Get to bed, child. A man of eighty-two has few enough pleasures as it is without being told what to eat."

Brandy turned abruptly and walked from the restaurant, intent on reaching the privacy of her room as quickly as possible. With a sigh of relief she opened her door after the brief elevator ride.

She switched on a bedside lamp, leaving the room in a dim golden glow. She was thankful that she was away from her godfather. The shock of seeing Brad had strained her nerves, and she knew it would take complete privacy to regain her former composure.

Within minutes she undressed and lay down in the huge bed. Tormented by her thoughts of Brad, she tossed and turned for hours until her headache was unbearable. Unable to sleep, she stood up, deciding to use the therapeutic powers of the hydra-massage unit.

The pool was maintained at the correct warmth and kept filled with sparkling clear water. The dim light from the bed lamp gave a definite coziness to the room, adding to its tranquillity.

Brandy removed her nightgown, pausing on the edge of the pool before easing into the soothing water. The contoured shape of the sleek porcelain was comfortable against her spine as she leaned back. Her eyes shut, she let the whirling water rush over her limbs in a relaxing aquamassage.

She slid lower into the pool, her vibrant hair pinned off her nape, soft warm water covering her to the top of her shoulders. With dismay she heard a click and the sound of a door opening and closing. She had latched the outer door, which made entrance through that door impossible. The only other possibility was the other door to the left of her bed. She had checked to see where it led but it had been securely locked. Frightened, she reached to turn off the aqua-massage unit before getting her towel when she saw Brad.

He towered in the doorway, pausing to look at her. He was clad in a short velour robe; his legs were exposed from the knee down, his well-sculpted calves covered with hair, the muscles taut and lean. His robe was carelessly belted around the waist, a thick mat of curly chest hair visible. The sudden awareness that the robe was his only covering broke her reverie.

"Get out, Brad."

"You expect me to leave after the trouble I went through to find you? Having you here was my intention, leaving you was not!" He stepped forward, casually removing his robe before stepping down into the water.

Brandy screamed out and started to leave the water, but Brad grabbed her ankle. One pull and she effortlessly slid toward him. "No, Brad . . . don't!"

"Come to me, Brandy."

"No. No, Brad. I can't." She twisted to get away, the water whirling around them in continuous motion. Desperate at the temptation filling her body, she squirmed.

"Quit struggling," Brad commanded arrogantly, his gaze hard.

Brandy, knowing she was clearly overpowered, tried to trick her captor. She pretended to offer no resistance until she felt Brad loosen his grasp, then she made her move.

Rising from the opaque security of the swirling water, Brandy was abruptly stopped. Brad's hands cupped her shoulders tenderly, a deep moan escaping his throat as he looked at her naked body.

His eyes were visible in the darkened room, their depths dilated as he stared at the beauty of her heaving breasts, the voluptuous curves rising and falling before she was pulled against his chest.

With a cry she surrendered to the excitement of his touch, her mouth responding as he parted her lips. His hunger was insatiable as he crushed her mouth. The savage caress was what she needed. In his arms she thought time stood still, his sensual expertise blotting out everything but his power over her senses.

Of their own accord her hands slid across his shoulders to his nape and drew his head close in order to deepen the kiss. She was drowning in sensuality—sweet, unbearable, erotic pleasure—as he continued to plunder her lips.

Stopped by her deep moans, afraid he had hurt her,

Brad reluctantly pulled his mouth a breath away, placing teasing kisses over her face as she whimpered with delight.

"Witch," he groaned, his mouth moving to her neck and ears. "Exciting, sweet, delectable witch. You've haunted my nights for weeks."

Breathless from Brad's uninhibited zeal, she gasped, "How did—did you find me?" Her weight rested on his outstretched legs, as her eyes gazed sensually into his.

"Shut up, Brandy. That's not important. Only this."

His mouth took hers again, the urgency of his desire communicated beneath her palms as she stroked his shoulders. "Always this, you witch." His kisses were driving her into a frenzy of need when he lifted her out of the water, his hands surrounding her rib cage as his mouth trailed downward before burrowing into the deep valley between her breasts. "Oh, God, you're absolutely beautiful. . . ."

As he held Brandy above him he lay back with his head resting on the edge. Bracing her slight weight easily, he moved her over him so his mouth had access to the enticing peaks of her full breasts. He took the nipples into his mouth and moaned at the pleasure of feeling them harden against his tongue. He sucked each erect tip in turn before trailing a sensuous path around her breasts. He nibbled on the satin-smooth burgeoning underside, then circled back eagerly to the rosy tips. Perspiration beaded his brow at her receptivity.

Brandy cried out at the erotic pleasure of his mouth, her stomach clenching at each flick of his firm tongue. Her sleek body trembled over his taut frame as the aqua-massage continued to agitate the water into foam, the pulsating rhythm matching her heartbeat.

"Stop . . . stop, Brad . . . please. I can't take any more," she cried out poignantly. "Don't love me anymore to-night."

"Don't?" he moaned against her breast, moving down to kiss the tender skin of her abdomen as he easily lifted her higher. "You actually have the courage to say don't?"

"Yes," she whispered, her body writhing, helpless against the strength of his large hands. "Yes . . . no . . . oh, don't stop."

Brad nipped her waist sharply before sliding her down the length of his body to cradle her against his chest. "That's better."

Breathless from his assault, Brandy burrowed into his neck. Her mouth lowered to kiss his broad chest as it rose and fell. "I—I was afraid you were going to make love to me in the water."

"Not at this temperature. I'm no sexual Adonis and water this hot makes it difficult. Now, if you want to turn the heater off or try the shower, that's another matter!"

"Quit teasing, Brad. We shouldn't be in here . . . un-clothed."

Brad laughed huskily. "You pick a hell of a time to act modest. I'm the man you gave your virginity to, remember?"

Brad eased upward, pulling Brandy with him after shutting off the massage unit. He stood unashamed on the carpeted floor, his nakedness as natural as if they had been living together for years.

Brandy felt helpless standing before him. Her desires waged a war with her morals as she stared at the masculine beauty of his intimidating body, thinking, *I want you, Brad. One more time, please.*

Head bowed, she turned her back, embarrassed by the desire to go to him again, to once more seek his love. She grabbed the soft bathsheet and wrapped it around her shoulders before turning around.

With great tenderness he pulled her forward, his hands gentle as he picked her up, her body still wrapped in the towel.

"You won't need that, Brandy," he whispered against her neck as he walked toward her bed. "You won't need anything but my arms, darling."

"But . . . how did you—"

"No questions tonight. How or why is unimportant to us now," he interrupted with a stark warning. He lay her onto the tumbled sheets, discarding the towel as he slipped in beside her. He drew her into his arms, his hands trembling as they began the exploration of her body.

Unable to resist a repeat of his tumultuous lovemaking, Brandy moaned. Her arms opened to clasp his back, a soft sigh of willingness wafting across his face as he bent to take her lips.

Brad's deep voice echoed across the room as he whispered his need for Brandy over and over, against her parted lips, closed eyelids, satiny cheeks, and sensitive earlobes until searing the pulsating warmth of her throat with his warm breath.

Without resistance she let him roll her onto her back, her limbs parting to receive him. Her eyes opened, tears trickling down her cheeks as she raised her arms to draw him down. Her need to give of herself was even stronger than it was in Las Vegas. The weeks apart had heightened their senses to unbearable ecstasy.

Brad leaned forward to cup her into his hold and end the pain of their unfulfilled desires.

"Are you happy, my witch?" he asked, his hands reaching to pull her hips to his body. "Happy to know you've cast an unbreakable spell over my senses?"

"Mmm . . ." she moaned against his throat. "What do you think?"

His breath fanned her mouth, his body shuddering above her as he held himself back from the moment of rapturous entry.

"I think you talk too much."

She arched upward, pushing against him, eager to accept his hardened body as he prolonged their coming together with strict control.

With a deep moan he lowered his hips, feeling her smooth thighs tremble uncontrollably when the harsh ringing of the telephone jarred their nerves. Automatically reaching for the receiver, Brad eased from Brandy's hold when he felt her hand on his back.

"Don't answer it, Brad. I'm supposed to be alone." It rang again as Brad handed it to Brandy. Lifting the receiver, she heard James's excited voice.

"Can you come down, Brandy? It's your godfather."

Alert, all passion leaving her body, she cried out, "What's the matter, James? He's all right, isn't he? He didn't have an attack?"

"No, nothing that serious. He's uncomfortable with pain from eating that rich pie. He knew he shouldn't have but he was his usual stubborn self. Now he can't sleep and wants you to come baby him."

Relieved that he would be fine, Brandy told James she would be down as soon as she dressed.

She set the receiver back, looking at Brad, who stood before her clad in his robe. His presence was a comfort. There was no reproach for the interruption of his passion, only concern for the well-being of her godfather.

·"Get dressed, Brandy. I'll put my clothes on, then we'll go take care of the colonel.".

He walked through the communicating door into his suite and closed it behind him to give her privacy to dress. Hastily slipping into a sweater and skirt, she brushed her hair to smooth out the telltale curls before opening the door into the hall.

Within seconds she was entering her godfather's suite and going straight to his room. Her heart went out to him as he lay propped up in bed, a guilty look on his face.

"Shame on you, Godfather. I'll wager you wish you hadn't eaten that pie now," she teased, sitting on the edge of the bed. She reached for his hand, and patted it as her voice soothed him.

"Wasn't Brad's pie. It was that darned place we ate lunch. I knew their food wasn't any good."

Brandy chuckled at his excuse and sudden defense of Brad's chef. Grateful, she looked up to see Brad come into the room dressed in casual slacks and a knit shirt. Her heart·went out to him. His presence seemed to fill the room with strength. For the first time Brandy could remember, she felt her worry about the colonel leave her shoulders. Like her godfather, she knew Brad would take care of all of them.

"How do you feel, Colonel?" Brad asked, standing beside the bed, his concern genuine.

"Not ready to lead a combat unit into battle, son."

"Well, my doctor will soon see you feel better, sir," Brad assured him. "He should be here within five minutes."

"How did you know I was ill, Brad?" the colonel asked, his face white, showing obvious pain.

"Brandy told me. Now, don't talk. We'll wait right here until you feel able to sleep."

"But what about your sleep?" the old man asked.

"I don't require much and I enjoy having someone to talk with at night." His eyes lingered on Brandy, aware of the deep circles beneath her eyes. Her shoulders slumped with fatigue as she held her godfather's hand, causing Brad's heart to wrench.

"As soon as Brandy is assured you'll be fine, we'll send her to her room. She looks worn out. Okay with you, sir?"

"Fine. Maybe she'll listen to you. She ignores everything I tell her."

"That's not so, Godfather!" Brandy retorted.

"See how she sasses me, Brad? I think I'll turn her care over to you. She needs a firm hand now and then."

Brad's eyes locked with Brandy's across the bed as he replied huskily, "That's fair enough. I think I can find some way to discipline her that won't be too uncomfortable to either of us."

A pink tinge colored Brandy's face as she looked away from Brad's piercing gaze. His subtle remark carried a warning that he was serious. She knew instinctively what his form of chastisement would take.

She left the room when Brad's doctor arrived, his rumpled clothing and mussed hair proving Brad had woken him. He returned to the living area after several minutes and assured Brandy that the old man would be fine. He had given him medication for his heartburn and something to make him sleep. By avoiding rich foods in the future, he should have no problems, the doctor told her before leaving.

Brad opened the bedroom door, motioning to Brandy

to come in. His hand rested on her shoulder as she walked beside him to the bed.

Her godfather lay resting, his eyes already lowering as he mumbled, "Go to bed, child. Brad agreed to stay with me tonight and I don't need you. We Marines know how to take care of each other."

With a cry Brandy knelt on the bed, clasping the old man to her. "I'm glad you're well, Godfather. I—I couldn't bear it if I lost you too!"

"Hush, child, and get to bed. You need your rest."

Brad nodded for Brandy to leave, his glance assuring her that her godfather would be well attended to for the balance of the night.

She smiled, her eyes filled with tenderness before leaving the bedroom, reminding James to get some rest before returning to her own room.

She prepared for bed in a daze. Brad's forceful personality had exerted itself throughout the evening. Too tired to think of the reasons for her contentment, she lay her head back against the pillow.

She pulled the covers around her face, the faint scent of Brad's after-shave a heady experience. The sheets were still slightly damp where he had lain beside her. She thought of their mutual hunger. It had been so strong, it seemed unnecessary for Brad to towel himself dry.

Within minutes Brandy was sound asleep, the deepest and most healing sleep since the loss of Daniel and Denise. Responsibility for her godfather's precarious health had been transferred to Brad's capable shoulders unconsciously. His willingness to assume charge was accepted without a single qualm.

CHAPTER FIVE

Brandy awoke slowly, stretching her limbs across the comfortable mattress. Happiness filled her at the thought of being with Brad each day for the next three weeks.

She had come to terms with her interest in him, no longer able to deny he had only to look at her to set her heart pounding. His touch was magic. She craved it as a man dying of thirst craves water.

She admitted it was partially due to constant self-denial during her marriage. Her body had matured along with her mind during the five celibate years with Daniel. The intensity of her response to each physical encounter with Brad was proof that her burgeoning womanhood and personal needs had been denied too long.

She had no foresight that her plan to become pregnant would include a personal involvement other than the one biological mating. It was only to be a coming together she was forced to endure for the sake of a modicum of affection in the years ahead. One intimate act in exchange for a child.

For a time the loss of her tiny daughter was more than she could endure. Her outpouring of love to Denise had given her life purpose. Her beautiful little girl had brought love and laughter into the lives of those around her. She had been a happy, contented baby from the moment she was born.

Brandy would never forget the tender protectiveness flooding her heart when she first held her infant daughter to her breast. She and Daniel had looked in awe at the tiny little girl with coal-black hair, unbelieving she was theirs to love and cherish.

Tears filled Brandy's eyes as she fought for composure. She compelled herself to believe there was a purpose in the tragedy.

The loss of Daniel and Denise were her past, their lives together now a memory. Her godfather's health was her immediate concern, Brad's reappearance a questionable future.

She sat up quickly when the door clicked open, heart beating wildly in anticipation of Brad's emergence. Her hair lay in tumbled curls around her shoulders; a soft flush tinged her cheeks as the door was flung back abruptly.

Brandy leaned against the headboard, speechless, as a small bundle of energy burst into her room, pockets filled with dust rags, hands pushing a vacuum through the doorway.

Without giving her time to comment she plugged it in and stood hands on hips, unashamedly staring at Brandy before cleaning the rugs.

"You're a lucky young woman to be Mr. Lucas's mistress," the maid told her bluntly. "He's very macho. All the women who stay here want him, chase him constantly, but he won't even look at them."

"But . . . I'm not his mistress!" Brandy blurted out, dismay crossing her face as the maid shook her head in disbelief.

"There's no need to deny it, dearie. You sleep in Mr.

Lucas's suite so . . ." She shrugged as if the matter was closed. "I see to them each day and this morning his bed was untouched."

"He stayed elsewhere last night!" Brandy retorted, mad at herself for bothering to make excuses to one of his staff. Her relationship with Brad was no one else's concern. Despite this she wished she could think of a plausible explanation for being there.

The loud hum of the motor as she vacuumed the carpeting prevented the need for conversation. Brandy turned back the covers and padded barefoot into the bathroom to dress. Clothes in hand, she sighed with relief that the door had a lock. She would have to see Brad about talking to his help. Any hint to her godfather that she was considered to be Brad's mistress could shock him into having another heart attack.

Wearing a white skirt and short-sleeve navy-blue blouse, she walked from the bathroom. Her makeup was expertly applied, hair brushed in smooth waves around her shoulders. As she took her sandals from the closet she heard the maid clucking like a mother hen as she made the bed.

Her darting fingers smoothed the sheets of the large bed. Both pillows were rumpled, as were the covers. To deny she had had company sometime during the night would be useless. She decided to gamble on her integrity and affection for Brad.

"I'm Brandy Harcourt, Miss—"

"Call me Anne, dearie," she said, expression curious as she patted the pillows into a smooth line.

"Thank you, Anne. I would like to ask you to keep a confidence for me if you would."

"Why sure, Miss Harcourt. I'm not one to gossip."

After smoothing the bedspread until it hung wrinkle free, she moved onto her dusting, the oiled rag flying over the heavy furniture with the competence of years of practice.

"Actually, Anne, I would appreciate you not telling another soul that I'm staying in Mr. Lucas's private suite. I'm here with my godfather and his valet and he would be shocked to learn about this arrangement. I hadn't realized myself this room was part of Brad's private suite."

Brandy slipped a couple of white bracelets over her wrist, her glance observing the pleased expression of the housekeeper.

"I understand. He's the old gentleman on the first floor whose health isn't too good. You can count on me to keep quiet, and I'll see the other girls don't talk either. Not that there are any secrets in a place like this, but we do know when to be discreet."

"Good, Anne. I knew I could count on you. Your face shows integrity," Brandy complimented her, liking her despite her bursting into the room unannounced and commenting on her and Brad's supposed actions.

"Are you responsible for the beautiful flowers and luscious-looking fruit?"

"Yes, Miss Harcourt. Do you like them? Mr. Lucas said you were to have the finest available. We've all been instructed to cater to the three of you."

"Good heavens! You certainly won't have to cater to us. We won't be any bother to anyone, if possible. Three weeks in this lovely resort to relax and get a tan is treat enough without special attention too."

Brandy picked up her purse prior to leaving the room, only to be stopped by Anne's voice whispering, "Don't worry, dearie. Mum's the word."

Brandy shut the outer door, deciding to walk to the

stairway. Her last glimpse was of a conspiratorial wink on Anne's homely face.

"Gosh, now I've done it again," Brandy murmured softly as she descended the wrought-iron stairway to the main floor. "By making a request not to say anything to the colonel, she assumes I'm guilty." She was in a turmoil as she walked toward her godfather's room. The scope of her indiscretion was widening. It was now more imperative than ever that she see Brad.

She knocked before entering the suite. Her godfather's door was open and he sat in bed, a tray across his lap. His look was smug as he smiled at her.

"Good morning, Godfather," she greeted him, a smile giving her face an ethereal beauty. "Did you sleep well?"

"Of course I did. Brad's doctor saw to that. I haven't felt so good in weeks." He took a drink of orange juice before eating another bite of his hot oatmeal.

"Have you eaten, Brandy?"

"No, not yet. I wanted to see how you were first." She looked around the room, curious about Brad's whereabouts but not wanting to inquire.

"I'm fine, I told you. Brad stayed with me all night, you know. Fine boy he is. Captain in the Marines, did I tell you?"

"Yes, Godfather. You told me. Er—where is he now?" she asked, unable to contain her curiosity any longer.

"Taking care of business. Won't be back until afternoon sometime. He wants me to try his mineral pool. He thinks the water might make me feel better."

"Wonderful, Godfather. I'll join you and start on my tan." Disappointment filled her at the thought that Brad was away. They needed to talk. She still had no idea how he found her or reassurance that he wouldn't mention their indiscreet affair in Las Vegas to her godfather.

"Did you and Brad talk last night?" she blurted out without thought.

Her godfather took his time answering, intent on chewing a bite of toast. His grizzled hair stood on end. He kept it cut short and it always stuck up despite the hair dressing he used to keep it smooth. It was a physical characteristic she admired affectionately. It made him appear vulnerable despite his gruff arrogance and demanding ways.

"Of course we talked, Brandy. I had lots of things I wanted to know about him, but he seemed more intent on finding out about you."

"Me?"

"Yes, you. Now go get your breakfast, then you can take me to the pool. James went to town to get me and him a bathing suit. He could use the mineral pool too beings he's almost my age."

"Godfather, shame on you. James is only sixty-five."

"Well, near enough to me, it don't count. Now get! Brad wants me in the pool before it gets too hot. It's already seventy-five degrees, you know."

Brandy reached forward, kissing his cheek before leaving for the coffee shop to get her own breakfast. She was filled with delight that the colonel seemed so fit. The change in him since her announcement that she was pregnant was hard to believe.

The thought of her pregnancy hit her hard. She had been so caught up in confronting Brad that it had slipped out of her mind. Her cheeks paled at him learning the news. He would know beyond a shadow of doubt it was his child. The consequence of her deception was fast getting beyond her ability to control.

Later that morning Brandy lay on a lounge in the shade of a colorful umbrella. She wore a white toweling robe over her bikini as she relaxed, uncertain yet whether she wanted to lay alone beside the swimming pool.

A smile crossed her face as she looked at James and the colonel. They sat in the heated water of the mineral bath, their eyes carefully avoiding contact with the number of older single women. Dressed in old-fashioned boxer-style suits, they contrasted distinctly with the skimpy skintight hip-hugging briefs worn by the younger men.

Brandy felt like a ghost as she eyed the deeply tanned skin of the people cavorting in the pool. She had thought her own bikini daring until she saw most of those worn by the other girls. They were merely strings, barely covering the essential parts of the body. From the back many women looked naked at first glance.

After placing a pair of dark glasses over her eyes to cut the glare from the pool, she lay back, letting the lethargic effect of the sun lull her into sleep. When James and the colonel told her they were going to their suite to relax, she acknowledged them with a nod, too relaxed to open her eyes.

She awoke with a start at the featherlight touch of lips teasing the corner of her mouth. Brad straightened up, his eyes filled with mirth as he towered over her.

"Quit that, you fool!" Brandy snapped, sitting up to glare at him for his intimate gesture while surrounded by dozens of people.

"As I recall from my fairy tale days, that wasn't what Sleeping Beauty said. Guess I better try again. Maybe I didn't do it right."

"Darn it, Brad," she hissed, looking to see if they could be overheard. "I'm not Sleeping Beauty and you're cer-

89

tainly no prince. You have no right to be so . . . intimate with me."

"No right? You've got to be kidding. From what I've learned about your past I'm the only man—including your husband of five celibate years—that has the right."

Brad sat on the edge of the cushioned lounge adjoining hers, wearing a white terry-cloth robe loosely tied. She was as aware of his physical magnetism as if he were unclothed. The sight of his strong knees, well-muscled calves, slender ankles, and long narrow feet caused her heart to thump wildly. He was tanned a deep bronze, the dark hairs on his legs and forearms barely visible. She wanted to reach out and trail her sensitive fingertips across his skin. To feel his steel-hard muscles quiver at her touch was a potent stimulus to her senses.

"Quit staring at me. Your eyes when you are aroused drive me insane. Already your gaze has lowered my intelligence quotient by half," he teased mischievously.

Brandy tore her glance from his face, turning her body sideways and slipping from the lounge to go to her room. Brad's teasing bothered her. His ability to interpret her thoughts with uncanny accuracy was even more of an embarrassment.

As she started to step forward she felt her wrist clasped. She turned to find Brad beside her, his long legs easily stepping over the lounge in order to prevent her from leaving.

"Weren't leaving, were you?"

"Yes, Brad. I've been in the sun enough today."

"You haven't been in the sun at all. You've been completely shaded by the umbrella plus that awful robe."

"My robe is exactly like yours!" she shot back, her eyes glittering as she raised her chin. He towered over her, his size intimidating; she stood barefooted on the patio, facing him mutinously.

Brad's eyes twinkled at her defiance, causing her tiny figure to shake with rage. "My robe is not covering a gorgeous body," he explained firmly. "Your figure puts every woman I've seen to shame. To cover it in a piece of toweling is a crime." His hands lifted and easily removed her robe, though she made a vain attempt to stop him.

"Horrible monster!" she sassed impudently before storming off to lay on a vacant poolside mattress. Facedown, hands crossed beneath her cheek, she was too irritated by Brad's arrogance to realize that every man around the pool was staring at her openmouthed.

Her rounded figure, exposed in cinnamon-toned bikini bottoms and plunging bra top, was eye catching. She was stunning. Small yet exquisitely proportioned, with shapely legs, curvaceous hips, minuscule waist, and high firm breasts that jutted upward to form deep cleavage. Her hair swung about her shoulders, its vibrant chestnut color contrasting with the luminous texture of her creamy skin.

Brad's eyes darkened, smoldering with unquenched desire caused by the unfinished turbulent lovemaking of their early-morning tryst. He removed his robe and threw it carelessly over hers on the lounge after removing a bottle of suntan lotion from the pocket. He noticed her satin-smooth skin and feared that exposure to the bright sun without protection would cause a painful burn. Any blemish to her flawless beauty should be prevented at all costs, he thought tenderly.

Brad walked forward, dragging a mattress along to lay down beside her. He set the lotion on it before scooting a table alongside, its umbrella casting streaks of shade over them. He kneeled on his mattress, pouring a capful of lotion into his palm before reaching toward her back.

Brandy kept her eyes shut, her dark glasses pushed upward over her hair. She'd heard the sound of Brad dragging the mattress toward her, had felt a swish of air as he dropped it beside her, even peeked long enough to see him dragging a table toward them, and felt the shadow of the umbrella cross her back.

His superior male attitude and dominance needed a setback, she thought. By refusing to utter a single word to him she would make him tire and leave. A smile tugged her lips as she contemplated getting the better of him, of proving that she would not permit him to subjugate her at will.

Brad saw her smile: he was aware of her belligerence but totally unperturbed. He leaned forward, his broad palms spreading the scented cream along her spine. With even strokes he smoothed it into her skin, his fingers gentle as they covered her back and shoulders. He felt her tremble as he untied the thin strap across her back and lay the ends alongside her breasts.

He ordered her to lay her arms alongside her body and, as she complied without protest, rubbed the cream into them. After pouring more lotion into his palms, he smoothed it over her legs, covering each inch from her ankles to her upper thighs.

Brad was becoming more inflamed by the second. His body responded to her sensuality without thought. He ached for her. The image of her beneath him and the memory of her uninhibited response that morning and in Las Vegas haunted each waking moment.

Brandy lay beneath the caressing motion of his hands, her composure lost the moment she felt the warmth of his broad palms. Her nerves screamed out for relief, his touch bringing ecstatic sensation as it trailed over her body.

When his hands left her limbs, she sighed with relief. She had forced herself to remain silent, had borne his seductive clasp without comment. With a shock she felt his hands return to her back, could feel the cooling lotion as he soothed it around her waist. Her breath caught as his fingers slid along her rib cage, the tips caressing the sides of her breasts crushed beneath her as she lay on her stomach. With his broad palms on her back he lingered, his fingers stroking the swell of her outer breasts. She could feel a deep trembling start in the pit of her stomach —a trembling of desire uncontrolled.

"You're quivering, little one. You feel it, don't you, Brandy? You want me as much as I want you."

"No . . . no, I . . . can't, Brad."

"Can't or won't?" he whispered, his voice husky with passion.

"Both. Don't you see? My only concern now is for the colonel. He could never understand my sudden interest in a stranger."

"Stranger? By God, I'm not that. I'm the man you sought. The man you beseeched to take you only a month ago. Just last night you were beneath me, your body arching to receive me."

"Don't. Please, don't say any more," she begged. Tears filled her eyes, trickling beneath the tightly clenched lids as she implored him to be quiet.

Heedless of her plea, his husky voice hissed against her ear as he leaned forward. "I want you. I want my hands over all of you—not just the parts exposed to everyone else's eyes. I want to touch your breasts, feel the nipples harden beneath my fingers. I want to rub my palms across your stomach and the smooth skin of your buttocks . . . let my fingers caress your inner thighs and upward."

"No, Brad," she cried out helplessly.

"Can you feel it, Brandy?" he continued relentlessly. "I can. The need for you is like a part of me now. It hurts so bad, this wanting you all the time."

Deep whimpers came from her throat as she listened, entranced.

"Come to your room. We'll make long, slow love on the bed until you're pleading with me to take you as you did in Las Vegas."

"No . . . no, Brad!" Her head shook and her body quivered beneath his hands as his words seduced her, their message as erotic as his touch as he retied her narrow bra straps.

With a cry of pain escaping her lips she stood up and rushed heedlessly to the pool to dive headlong off the side into the deep cold water. Brad had aroused her to the point that she forgot everything other than her need—dormant needs that had surfaced with the force of a volcano.

An excellent swimmer, she continued across the pool, intent on reaching the other side to climb out and rush to her room. If necessary she would lock herself in the bathroom until it was time to have dinner with her godfather. Anything to avoid Brad's hypnotic words and physical presence.

Nearing the side she felt a hand clasp her ankle, stopping her beneath the water to pull her under against his broad powerful body.

At the first touch she knew it was Brad. She felt helpless against his forceful strength, yet she struggled determinedly. She managed to fight her way upward, breaking the surface, gasping for air, dark hair streaming around her face in long wet strands.

Brandy shook water from her eyes, her face inches from Brad's. His pitch-black hair was slicked down across his head; his eyes were consumed with unrequited passion. She cried out at the look as his head descended to claim her mouth.

Lips clinging, arms and legs entwined, they sank beneath the surface in the deep end of the pool. The blue water distorted their image to the interested eyes of the people watching. Passion sizzled as they slowly drifted upward, mouths still clinging, their lungs ready to burst.

Gasping for air, Brandy clung to his neck, too weak to protest as he held her close. He paddled to keep them on the surface while they tried to regain enough composure to leave the pool.

Brandy pushed her wet face into his throat, her tears mingling with the pool water as she whimpered, her emotions in complete havoc.

"How could you, Brad? It would kill my godfather to see me in the arms of another man."

Brad swam to the edge of the pool, his hands holding her against the side, his body pushing forward to rub against her sleek wet skin. "He won't see us. I stopped to visit him before I came to you. He's taking his nap now."

The touch of Brad's body and the sight of water running through the mat of hair on his broad chest continued to torment her. She put her mouth against his shoulder, biting the taut muscle near his neck in a sensuous manner. The taste of chlorinated water was strong, but nothing mattered except his continued touch.

Attention left them as a rowdy game of water volleyball began across the pool. The unexpected passionate kiss under water was forgotten. Brandy sighed with relief, her cheeks still rosy with embarrassment. Brad remained aloof, totally unconcerned whether they had an audience or not.

Worried that her godfather might observe her, Brandy pulled back. Brad rained kisses across her throat before burrowing his face in the wet strands of hair. He nibbled possessively on her neck and ear, arrogantly ignoring her futile protests.

"Stop, Brad. What if James should see you?" She pushed against his shoulders, her touch ineffectual on the wet skin.

He nipped her earlobe before probing her ear with his tongue, a caress that caused her stomach to knot with desire.

"You like that, huh?" he teased, doing it again until she writhed away from his hold.

She turned on him, venting her fury at his refusal to leave her alone. "Damn you, Brad! James may be watching us this very moment."

"So what? I already told him I love you and intend to make you my wife."

"You *what*?" she hissed in disbelief at his audacity.

"You heard me," he explained calmly. His arms snaked out, pulling her into his hold, forcing her to reach for his neck in order to keep from being dunked beneath the water. He cupped her face in his broad palms, his elbows hooked on the inside handhold to keep them afloat as he growled at her.

"Shut up, woman, and enjoy this."

Her eyes darkened, hands clinging to his broad shoulders as she relaxed. At that moment she didn't care if anyone saw them and she parted her lips to receive his kiss. His mouth opened, and his tongue probed her teeth until she accepted the deepening kiss with equal passion.

They sank beneath the surface for the second time. As Brad's feet touched bottom he pushed upward and they surfaced with a swirl of water splashing around them. Helpless against his expertise, Brandy clung to his neck and let him pull her slight weight to the side of the pool.

Brad hopped out lithely, then bent to assist Brandy from the water. With his hand clasped around her waist he led her to their robes. He was aware of her capitulation as he placed her robe around her shoulders before pulling his own on. Holding her waist, he guided her possessively to the entrance, where they went in complete silence to her room.

He kissed her tenderly on the forehead, opening her door to push her inside, closing it behind her so she could have the privacy that she needed so desperately.

Brad's physical assault had left her depleted of energy. He could feel her weariness and knew if he left her she would rest. He thought that best for now. She was his. That's all that was important now. He could wait.

Brandy entered the cozy room listlessly. She walked to the bathroom to take a cool shower, knowing instinctively Brad would not appear. With scented shampoo she washed the damaging chlorine out of her hair. Her skin had already regained a faint tan.

Dressed in gold pajamas, she sat on the bed, toweling her silky hair until it was dry. It glistened with luxuriant life across her shoulders as she crawled into bed totally bewitched.

She was asleep instantly, face cradled by the soft pillow, her slight form barely a mound beneath the sleek satin sheets.

CHAPTER SIX

At six o'clock Brandy took a final look in the bathroom mirror. Her image reflected an impeccably groomed woman with subtle makeup and gleaming hair brushed into soft waves across slender shoulders, clad in a new dress that emphasized a petite figure.

She twisted a lustrous curl on each side of her cheek before adding a spray of Cinnabar by Estée Lauder to her wrists, throat, and beneath her ears. Its scent matched the sophistication of her dress. The ecru floral lace with tucked bodice, winged collar and cuffs was utterly feminine. Its soft skirt flared to her knees from a tightly belted waist.

A classic set of matched pearls circled her throat, a birthday gift from her godfather. Handmade Italian spike-heeled sandals with dainty straps at the ankle and toe clung to her small feet as she walked to the elevator.

In the lobby she turned toward the sumptuous lounge when she saw her godfather and Brad relaxing at the bar. As her godfather continued his conversation Brad looked up, their eyes meeting across the room.

He stood, his expression enigmatic, watching her walk forward. Her fingers trembled in his hand as he clasped them to assist her onto a stool. She knew his thoughts, like hers, were on their first meeting.

"Good evening, Brandy," he greeted her huskily. "You look beautiful tonight. Don't you agree, Colonel?" he asked, turning to her godfather for confirmation.

"Brandy's always beautiful to me, Brad. But, yes, she does seem to have an added sparkle tonight. It must be this healthy desert air."

"Possibly," Brad confirmed, his breath catching as he inhaled the seductive scent of her perfume. "Will you join us in a drink before dinner?" he asked, motioning to the attentive bartender before she had time to answer.

"Yes. I think I'll have amaretto and cognac with soda and a lime wedge on the rocks." A smile tugged her lips as she watched Brad's expression change. "Surely you didn't think I'd order a Shirley Temple, Mr. Lucas," she teased, enjoying the opportunity of exchanging words when he could not retaliate. Her godfather's presence had distinct advantages, she thought smugly.

Brad's brow raised as he ordered her drink. The fact that he made no comment warned her he would settle with her impudence later that night.

He sipped his drink as the colonel continued telling him about numerous exploits during his lengthy military career. Brandy listened quietly, knowing contentment because she was with the two men she loved. Her glass hit the counter with a thud, and her face paled at the admission. She clenched her lashes, crying inwardly at the thought that she had allowed herself to fall for Brad.

She had vowed years ago that she would never allow herself to be subject to the emotional upheaval of caring for a man again. Her marriage to Daniel had brought her close to a nervous breakdown before she reconciled herself to accepting their problems. She had loved Daniel, but he had not had the capability of touching the depths of her heart.

Her fingers trembled in her lap as she thought of Brad. He had not only touched her heart, he had claimed it exclusively that unforgettable night in his Las Vegas hotel suite. He had received her love as well as her virginity, a fact she had steadfastly refused to acknowledge until their eyes locked across the bar as she walked toward him.

Brandy remained silent, head bowed, too devastated to even finish her drink. She felt Brad's hands clasp her fingers covertly as he bent to her ear.

"It's about time," he whispered. "It happened to me a month ago."

She raised her face, forgetting her godfather sitting on the other side of Brad. Her eyes filled with tears as he smiled at her. The love in their depths caused her heart to overflow with happiness. His extrasensory perception of her thoughts continued to amaze her. Throughout her years with Daniel they had never touched each other's soul.

"What do you think about that, Brad?" her godfather interrupted them, displeased that Brad had turned away from his conversation.

"Oh, fine . . . fine, sir," he answered, his attention returning to the colonel, trusting his noncommittal answer would suffice.

"Good, son. We'll go eat, then tomorrow you can drive us around to look at your city."

"Excellent, Colonel. It will be my pleasure." He took Brandy's arm to escort her to the dining room, the colonel following behind, his back ramrod stiff despite his age.

They relaxed in the padded booth while Brad ordered.

When he handed her a pair of dark glasses, Brandy looked up. She smiled in remembrance before flushing at his mischievous teasing.

"I think these are yours, Brandy. They were found at the bottom of our swimming pool. The deep end to be exact. Apparently they fell off while you were sunbathing. Do you have any idea how they could have got into the water?"

"No doubt some ruffian knocked them into the pool," she returned, a smile giving her face a look of complete innocence.

"No doubt," Brad agreed, laughing.

"That's hard to believe, Brandy. I haven't seen anyone acting out of line since I've been here," the colonel interrupted without looking up as he crumbled a handful of crackers in his soup.

"While you were asleep today, Godfather, there was a problem with one of the men. He bothered one of the young girls so much, she had to leave the pool area."

Brad's thighs pushed against her as he slid to the side before reaching under the table to grip her knee in a ruthless hold.

"You should have let me know who he was, Brandy. I would have had him thrown out," Brad taunted, his hand lingering on her thigh, forcing her to endure his caress without making a protest.

"No problem, Brad. The girl seemed capable of handling the situation quite well." Her sharp heel stamped his toe for emphasis.

"Hush, here comes our prime rib," her godfather said, wanting to eat. His appetite had improved tremendously since arriving at Casa del Oro. He seemed intent on making up for the meals he missed during his post-funeral depression.

Brandy watched as a serving cart was wheeled to the table. Succulent prime ribs of beef were sliced to their choice and served with baked potato heaped with sour cream and chives and fresh steamed brocoli.

Trivial conversation was exchanged throughout the excellently prepared meal. As Brandy tasted a spoonful of fresh strawberry shortcake topped with rich whipped cream, she dreamed about her relationship with Brad, their unfaced obstacles ignored.

"Will you go horseback riding with me tomorrow before daybreak? The beauty of the sun rising over the desert will leave you speechless," Brad whispered, his eyes lingering on her mouth as if anticipating its touch later that night.

"Of course!" Brandy exclaimed happily. "I adore riding. I belonged to Flintridge Riding Club for years—"

"Sorry, Brad," the colonel interrupted gruffly. "Apparently Brandy forgot. She can't ride now. Too dangerous."

"Why?" Brad asked with concern, looking from one to the other.

"Good heavens, son, haven't we told you yet? She's pregnant."

Brad went completely still, his expression one of utter astonishment. Pregnant? Brandy was going to have *his* baby? He couldn't believe it. She had told him she was taking the pill. Had she deliberately prevented him from protecting her to conceive a child? Impossible! No woman would seek to conceive a stranger's baby, he rationalized. Besides, she hadn't even known he was wealthy or cared to find out where he lived. That ruled out blackmail. I can't believe what's happening, but if she's having my

103

child, she'll damn well take my name. No son or daughter of mine will be born illegitimate.

The sudden silence was heavy. Brandy felt faint, blood leaving her face in a rush. She could feel Brad's shock, his body tensing beside her.

His knuckles were white as he gripped the edge of the table, before speaking in a low clipped voice. "I didn't know that. A definite oversight on Brandy's part. How far along are you, if I may be so forward as to ask?" His head turned, eyes dark smoldering charcoal, pinning her as he awaited an explanation.

"I—I'm—" Brandy stuttered, her eyes lowered to her lap, unable to even look at Brad.

"Good Lord, Brandy, quit dithering. It's not like you to mumble," her godfather scolded before looking at Brad. "She's not too far along, Brad. Told me preceding this trip that she got pregnant right before the accident."

"How tragic for you," Brad mocked as he relaxed against the booth, watching her discomfort without sympathy.

"Not tragic at all. I hope she has another child exactly like Denise. She was the image of my son. He had pitch-black hair and smoke-gray eyes just like his daughter's— and, come to think of it, just like yours. Most unusual in our family since we're all blue-eyed blondes."

"How lucky for him," Brad replied smugly. A sarcastic expression crossed his face as he glanced at Brandy.

"It was this news that snapped me out of my depression, son. I didn't want to live until Brandy told me she was pregnant. That and your offer to stay here with your excellent facilities is what made the difference. Now I feel like I could go on for years."

104

"I certainly hope you do, Colonel. I'll be interested in seeing this grandchild of yours myself."

Brandy was unable to stand the continued torment of not knowing whether Brad would blurt out the news of her indiscretion. She looked anxiously at her godfather, who was finishing a dish of bland milk custard and grumbling under his breath that he couldn't have an éclair instead. Misery was reflected in her eyes as she pleaded, "Excuse me, please. I'm—I'm suddenly feeling faint."

Brad rose from the booth and assisted Brandy from the table before looking at the colonel, his hand gripping her arm mercilessly.

"Excuse us both, Colonel. What Brandy needs is fresh air. If you don't mind, I'll take her for a short drive."

"No. No!" Brandy blurted out, making a futile attempt to free her arm without being conspicuous.

"Go on, child," her godfather insisted. "Do you good to get away. It's time for my checker game with James anyway. Brad will see you're well taken care of, won't you, son?"

"I will see that Brandy gets all the attention a woman in her condition deserves, sir. You can count on it."

Without giving Brandy time to kiss her godfather good night or think up an excuse to avoid his company, Brad had rushed her to the parking lot. Within seconds she was seated in the luxurious front seat of a powerful Lincoln Continental.

She could feel Brad's anger as he maneuvered through the busy main street of town before heading toward the hills.

"Brad . . . I—"

"Be still! I'm too damn mad to listen to you prattle now.

105

You can sit there and think up another scheme or some more lies while I drive to our destination!"

"I was only—"

"Shut up, dammit! I'm so infuriated with you, I could ring your satiny little neck. For your sake and the sake of dear sweet Daniel's unborn baby, you'd better do as I say, you lying witch."

Brad pulled to the side of a paved winding road, his tires screeching as he ground the heavy car to a halt.

Brandy pressed against the corner, eyes wide with fear as Brad turned sideways. A scream caught in her throat when he reached for her left hand, viciously removing the platinum wedding band from her finger.

"Stop. . . . What are you doing?" she cried out as he pressed the button to lower his window.

"What I should have done the first time I saw it." Brad threw her ring into the night, then pulled forward with such force, she was jarred against the seat.

Tears filled her eyes as she huddled helplessly in the corner, waiting for him to stop. His anger was like a living thing, filling the car with tension as he continued along the winding highway.

She swallowed back a sob, determined he wouldn't see the pain his sudden animosity caused. She watched curiously as he stopped before ornate wrought-iron gates set in an adobe wall. Electrically controlled, they opened at a touch of a button inside his car.

"Where—where are you taking me?"

"My home," he ground out, his voice harsh. "And be still. You'll have plenty of time to make your excuses known when we're in the privacy of my living room."

Brandy sat quietly, awed by what she could see in the floodlights placed at intervals along the drive. She had no idea Brad had a home other than his suite at Casa del Oro. It was obvious his wealth far surpassed that of her own fortune and her godfather's affluence combined.

His huge home sprawled across a hilltop overlooking Palm Springs. She had seen brief glimpses of the city as he drove up the long private road to his well-secured entrance.

Brad parked beneath a wide covered patio, then turned to look at her in the glare of his porch light.

"This is it Your time of reckoning has arrived." His eyes were narrowed, his look murderous. He eased his body from the comfort of the car's cushioned leather seat, slammed the door, then walked to her side, reaching for the handle to open her door.

Brandy remained seated, her head turned to avoid his scornful glance. Her heart beat like a wild thing in fear of what he would do when he found out the full implication of her deceit. She had no doubt he would be angered beyond reason—it showed in the clenching of his knuckles and taut jaw as he sped to his home.

"Get out!"

"N-no," she whispered, hands clasped tightly in her lap to control their trembling.

Brad reached into the car and picked up her struggling body effortlessly. He carried her without comment into his home as she writhed to break his painful hold.

"Quit struggling, damn you. Despite your scheming, devious little mind, I don't intend causing you pain." Crushed to his wide chest, she was carried through his service entrance and kitchen into an enormous living room.

He set her on her feet, his eyes holding her glance as she

tried to regain a modicum of self-possession. His deep voice was a warning as he spoke in a furious manner.

"Start talking, Brandy. I want to hear every single damn thing about you. From the moment you purchased that ridiculous blond wig at I. Magnin's in Pasadena to the day you received my invitation."

"But—but how did you know I bought it there?" she asked, her eyes wide with disbelief that he had traced her through the wig.

"That's my business. Start talking, and when I'm satisfied you're telling the truth about that, you can backtrack and tell me everything about your . . . marriage, Daniel, and your child."

Brandy turned from him, her eyes filled with pain, as she walked around the living room. She didn't know where to begin. Brad's anger intimidated her. She feared what form his punishment would take when she refused to explain a single point of her marriage and birth of her child. Her vows of secrecy had been made years earlier. She had no immediate thought of betraying them.

"Cat got your tongue?" Brad mocked, walking to a deep chair, sized to hold his powerful body comfortably. He sank into the cushions, relaxing with one elegantly clad foot resting across his knee and his hands gripping the arms of the chair, waiting for her to speak.

"I—I don't know where to start," she cried out, pacing back and forth across the deep-pile carpet in front of him, gesturing nervously with her hands.

"Sit down, for God's sake! Like I told you, start at the beginning."

Brandy looked over his living room, indifferently registering its contemporary elegance in her nervousness. Soft couches in russet velour formed a broad U. Plush square pillows in earth tones from ecru to chocolate leaned against the corners. Wall to wall carpeting, thick enough to sink in, was a deeper shade of russet. Beamed ceilings of imported woods coordinated with the simple lines of his furniture.

A massive fireplace jutted into the room, its chimney rising majestically to the ceiling. The rough-textured adobe bricks were startling white, as were the sheer drapes pulled to each side of the wide picture window opposite the fireplace.

Indian baskets were filled with a profusion of green plants from dracaena palms to split-leafed philodendrons. An extensive gun collection was displayed, along with objets d'art from around the world. The room was so massive, each thing complemented the other without a feeling of clutter. It was a masculine room but one that beckoned with warmth and comfort.

A sudden feeling of weakness overtook her as she sat across from Brad. She felt strained, her complacence gone the moment her godfather blurted out she was pregnant.

"Relax, Brandy. Kick off your shoes and sit back. You have all the time in the world. I intend to keep you here until I find out all I want to know. Whether it takes one night or ten makes no difference to me," he warned her, controlling his impatience by force.

Doing as Brad suggested, she curled her feet beneath her, resting her back against the velvety cushions.

Irritated by her continued silence, Brad blurted out furiously, "How could you possibly rationalize coming to me only three weeks after your husband's death without showing any sign of grief?"

Tears shimmered in Brandy's eyes as she faced him with

a sudden surge of spirit. "I had to. It was that night or not at all."

"You had to? Why the hell did you have to? My God, I doubt if I could ever make love to another woman again if you died. To do so in only twenty-one days is sacrilegious!"

"Not if the only alternative was a lifetime without love. Can't you understand?" she cried out, her hands raised in a pleading gesture. "I missed my baby so terribly, I was so lonely. I came to you that night knowing it was my only opportunity to get pregnant."

"Only opportunity? You're only twenty-six years old. You have years yet to conceive a child."

"Not—not if I was to pass it off as Daniel's child. I was desperate that my child should be legitimate. Unless I got pregnant within a month of Daniel's death, no one would believe it was his child. A second marriage was abhorrent."

"You were so determined, that any man would do? I was picked solely because I was in the right place at the right time?" he mocked, his eyes blazing into hers.

"No. Not for . . . that reason alone."

"Then why? Tell me why before I come over there and vent my anger by taking your body until you cry for mercy . . . then take you again and again until I'm as impotent as Daniel!"

Brandy bowed her head to hide her shame. Dark lashes formed crescents against her pale cheeks as she whispered, "I—I picked you because you had black hair . . . and gray eyes." She refused to refute his comments about Daniel.

Brad muttered a series of oaths as he rose from his chair in a bound. He was the one to pace the carpet now, his right hand rubbing the back of his neck as he contemplated her words. He stopped abruptly, looming over her.

"You picked me because I had dark hair and the right color eyes?"

"I thought it would assure that no one doubted it was Daniel's. If my second child had the same coloring as Denise—my daughter had."

"Quit calling Denise your daughter! You never had a child!" He rubbed his forehead to ease the sudden throbbing pain across his temples before blurting out bluntly, "My God, Brandy, you never even had a lover before we met. Whose child was she? Tell me!" he demanded, his voice piercing loudly through the silent room.

"No! Never! I came to you because I wanted another baby. That is all you ever need to know," she shouted defiantly, hands raised in anguish.

"You damn liar. You told me you were on the pill!"

His voice seared her, the escalating anger filling the room, making it close in around her.

"You deliberately gave yourself to me to get pregnant. I could understand it more if you were in need of physical release. But no. You only put up with sex for the purpose of having something to smother with frustrated motherhood for the years ahead." He turned on her, his broad shoulders shaking in his wrath. "If you wanted something to cuddle, why the hell didn't you buy a damn teddy bear!"

Tears streamed down Brandy's cheeks and her shoulders drooped in humiliation while Brad continued to berate her. His wrath forced her to admit how unthinking she had been.

Her reasons were selfish. She wanted a child to appease her loneliness, refusing to look ahead to the years it would be deprived of the guidance of its rightful father.

111

"Quit crying, dammit! You're only adding to your appearance of instability," he admonished her bitterly.

"I—I can't help it," she sobbed uncontrollably.

Brad stopped, hands clenched into tight fists at each side of his hips as he stood with legs splayed in front of her cowering form.

"Did it never even occur to you that your actions were dangerous? You could have gone to a room with a pervert, a masochist, or white slaver."

"White slavery went out with high button shoes!" she shot back, facing him with a sudden spurt of angry pride.

"My God, how very young you are. You're too damn naive to run around loose. Do you actually believe man's needs have been refined to the point that he wouldn't kidnap a nubile female to satisfy his depravities before forcing her to submit to other sickies he procures?"

Brandy's face went deathly white at the implication of Brad's words. She had never even considered that aspect in her haste to become pregnant within a month of Daniel's death.

"You foolish woman. My God, but you were ripe for attack. You're stunningly gorgeous with a figure that arouses men's baser instincts. Besides, you're so damn small, you couldn't defend yourself against a nine-year-old boy!"

"I—I could so," she blurted out irritably.

"Prove it!" Brad growled, gripping the nape of her neck with his right hand and pulling her from the couch. He dragged her forward, his head descending to take her mouth. His left arm remained at his side as he held her pressed against the length of his strong body.

Brandy writhed desperately in a vain attempt to free herself. His hand tightened while she beat ineffectually against his hard body with her knotted fists. She attempted to raise her knee to no avail. Whimpers were torn from her throat as he continued with his erotic punishment, plundering ruthlessly, his tongue parting her lips in a deep, angry kiss.

At the sound of her pitiful cries Brad stopped and released her. He thrust her quivering body from him with scornful words.

"See what an easy mark you'd have been? I controlled you effortlessly with one hand. I could have stripped you naked, raped and thrown you out of my suite without leaving a mark on your body. You're as helpless against a man's strength as the baby you went to so much trouble to conceive."

Touching her throbbing lips, Brandy whispered brokenly. "I—I never thought. But it probably wouldn't have mattered anyway. I wanted desperately to get pregnant and I needed a . . . man."

Brad interrupted her savagely. "You little witch. You used me as a damn stud. Any man with the right coloring would have done as well."

"No . . . no, that's not true," she cried out. "I went to three other hotels in Las Vegas. I had been looking for hours but couldn't do it. I found several suitable men."

"Why me?"

"I'm not certain. I was desolate by then. Ready to abandon my plan. I didn't even know your eyes were gray until I sat down beside you."

"You expect me to believe that?" he retorted scornfully.

The honesty in her eyes compelled him to listen despite his suspicion that she was not telling the truth. He watched her closely through narrowed eyes as she raised her hands in pleading.

"It's the truth, Brad. When I walked into that lounge, my eyes were drawn to you. It was like you were meant to be there for me. Your size and physical appearance commanded me to come forward. When I walked to you, it was as if an inner peace settled over me."

Brandy walked forward and placed her hands on Brad's arms, beseeching him to understand her desperate state of mind in Nevada. "I thought you were perfect," she told him in a soft, dreamy declaration.

Brad towered over her as she stood in stockinged feet. Her flawless beauty and clear, innocent eyes, compelling him to listen sympathetically, brought a negative reaction. Brandy had deceived him in Las Vegas, had left his suite without giving him the opportunity to express his sudden love. She had lied to her beloved godfather. Yet she expected him to overlook her indiscretion despite his weeks of angry indignation having to search for her.

Brad raised his hands to cup her face in his broad palms as their eyes locked. "You must think me stupid to believe your story. Thanks to years of indoctrination into the arts of trickery from your sex, I've become less gullible than I might have been twenty years ago. Sorry, Brandy, but I don't buy your tale of woe."

"It's true, Brad," she cried out, her hands touching his waist as she moved against him. "It was only with you I felt I could be . . . intimate. I didn't know we would ever meet again or the anguish and pain our tryst would cause."

"Pain and anguish for whom?"

"For me. You knew I was innocent that night. After I arrived home, my distress and agony began. The long weeks we've been apart proved how much my plan backfired. I've been so unhappy, Brad," Brandy cried out,

114

pressing her face into his chest, expecting him to comfort her as he had in the past.

Brad's back was rigid as she clung to his waist, his arms holding her loosely. "Why?" he ground out grimly. "Why were you so unhappy?"

Brandy looked at the planes of his face, his narrowed eyes, and rigid jaw. Her eyes were tormented, their amber color a deep velvet as she cried out poignantly, "Because I was certain I would never see you again. You plagued my dreams each night, my thoughts each day. Don't you even believe that I love you now?"

"No!" Brad exclaimed harshly, his hands gripping her shoulders in a viselike hold. "The only thing I'm certain of is that you were a virgin when we first met. My personal opinion is that after five years of a marriage without sex you were climbing the walls with frustration."

"No . . . no, that's not true. I—"

"Shut up," Brad interrupted, continuing with his diatribe. "When you couldn't hold out any longer, you came to Las Vegas looking for some stud—any man would do—to give you what your dead husband no longer could and apparently when alive felt wasn't worth the effort."

Brandy's hand flew up of its own accord and slapped Brad's jaw with all the strength she had. Her face was white with shock, her eyes darkened with mortification from Brad's unexpected insult.

She wrenched to escape his hold, unable to spend an another moment in his presence. "Take me home. I'll leave first thing in the morning. I never want to see you again as long as I live."

Bitter tears fell from her eyes as he released her. She stumbled toward the entrance, putting on her sandals, intent on returning to the hotel even if she had to walk.

115

"Not seeing me as long as you live will be pretty hard since we're going to be married in the morning," he told her calmly, his glance lingering on her stiffened back.

With a composure she thought beyond her capability she turned to face him, quivering chin held proudly high.

"I wouldn't marry you, Brad, if you were the last man on this earth. I just had a tragic ending to five years of marriage that in the beginning nearly cost me my sanity. Do you have the gall to imagine that I would turn immediately around and marry a man who has insulted me as you just did?"

Admiration for her spirit filled him as he watched her attempt to put him in his place. Unperturbed, he told her with added emphasis, "You heard me right the first time. With or without your consent we will be married tomorrow."

"You can't marry me without my consent," she warned him, her back straight and her eyes flashing sparks of fury. "And that, Mr. Brad Lucas, you will never get!"

"Wouldn't like to wager on that, would you?"

"Certainly!"

"You'd lose."

"I most certainly would not. You have no hold over me."

"I have several holds over you," he interposed quickly. "One: your devotion to your godfather. That I have no doubt is genuine. For some reason, which I will investigate later, he is convinced that your marriage was normal and that his son, Daniel, fathered a second child."

Brandy's control faltered, her face losing its color for the second time as she sensed what was to come.

"Two: the colonel's health is bad. I have medical evidence that he has a severe heart condition."

116

"You wouldn't!" Brandy cried out weakly, afraid she would faint waiting for his next words.

"Three," he continued, his eyes hard and steady. "If he knew of your indiscretion, there is the distinct possibility it would kill him."

"Oh, no . . . you couldn't," she wept, tears falling freely down her cheeks as she slumped into the nearest chair. She felt faint, filled with disbelief that her deception could actually lead to this final ultimatum.

"I want you, Brandy. I want you as my wife. My first child will not be born without its rightful heritage from its natural father."

"I can't, Brad. Can't you see why? Do anything you want to me. Punish me, scorn me, and insult me, but for the love of God don't force me to marry you now. The colonel would never understand."

Brandy lowered her head and cupped her face in the palms of her hands as she cried unashamedly. "I love him, Brad. I—I couldn't bear to ever cause him grief."

"You tell the colonel or I will," Brad retorted impatiently, his eyes hard and steady, expression formidable.

"I can't," she sighed in a deeply moving voice.

"Let's go, then. I'll take you back to your room. I'll find out later about your . . . marriage. I think we've both had enough turmoil for one night."

"But . . . what about—"

"Tomorrow we get married, that's what about. We'll take my jet to Nevada and be back here to start our honeymoon a few hours later."

"Give me thirty days," Brandy pleaded. "At the end of one month I'll tell him . . . everything."

"I'll agree to three weeks on one condition." Brad nodded.

117

"What?"

"That during those twenty-one days you will do anything I want." His eyes flicked over her threateningly. "I will promise that during the three weeks the colonel will not have the slightest suspicion of our compromise."

"What will you expect of me?" she asked warily.

"Whatever I want, you bestow. When I'm in the mood, I'll take you. When I'm not, you will be free to spend time with your godfather."

"That's inhuman. Slavery was abolished years ago!" she blurted out impulsively.

"It's your fault. You came to Las Vegas. You picked me to be your partner. Your uninhibited response and sensual prowess, despite your being virtuous, has tormented my mind since we first met. Now it's your turn to ease the frustrations caused by your devious scheme."

With emphasis he informed her seriously, "I will be discreet to a degree but I damn well won't bother to make an appointment ahead of time when I want you."

Brandy resisted as he reached for her, angering Brad further. She felt herself pulled into his arms, her head bent backward as he lowered his mouth to take her lips in a long savage kiss. Despite his insults and her worry about the revelations she would have to make in three weeks, her arms clung to him, eager to abandon herself to each caress. Angry or not.

Brad crushed her to his chest, pulling her upward until her toes barely touched the rug, her body pressed against the full length of his. One hand cupped the swell of her breast, the other spread across her spine.

Desire from her melting resistance filled him as he parted her lips to explore the heady moistness inside. The thought of possessing her body anytime he wanted provoked a trembling surge of sexual urgency he suddenly found impossible to control.

As Brad released her mouth Brandy slumped dejectedly, fingers clinging to his shoulders to keep from falling. Her legs threatened to collapse after the physical onslaught she had just experienced.

Brad had used her mouth ruthlessly, his anger finding release in the punishment of her lips. Brandy raised her hand to touch her swollen lips with a tentative finger. They felt bruised and she could taste blood, not knowing if it came from her mouth or his during the merciless kiss.

Brandy caught a brief flash of remorse in Brad's eyes before he looked away. He appeared to be deep in thought, his hand once again gentle as he placed it on her waist to lead her through the kitchen area to his waiting car.

They were silent as he drove back to Casa del Oro. Brad parked in front of the main entrance, then courteously escorted her to her room. He took a master key from his slacks pocket, opened her door, then stood aside for her to enter.

Brandy hesitated, uncertain whether he planned to stay with her that night. She looked at him, face tinged with embarrassment, contemplating what to say.

As usual he read her thoughts accurately. "No, Brandy. Not tonight," he said in a voice husky with sudden compassion.

He lowered his head to place a brief featherlight kiss on her bruised mouth.

Brad's face blurred as her eyes filled with tears. She knew she was more capable of keeping her composure when he was angry than she could ever do when he treated her with tenderness. She heard a deep moan escape his

119

throat before his arms enfolded her within their softening hold.

Brad buried his face in the silken strands of lustrous hair that framed Brandy's tragic face. He inhaled its familiar scent with pleasure. His hands slid the length of her spine, stroking slowly up and down. Brushing her hair aside, he kissed her neck and ear in despair over his actions.

Brandy heard a deep, husky whisper—a painful declaration of love that seemed torn from his very soul. Suddenly he broke away and left the room.

In a daze, her mind reeling from the poignant words murmured by Brad, she walked slowly toward the bathroom. Her preparations for bed were automatic. The sheets felt blessedly cool against her limbs, bared below a thigh-length lacy gown, the touch a welcome change from the heated anger of Brad's earlier confrontation.

Brandy drifted into a restless sleep, knowing her torment was not that he would take her when he wanted . . . but that he might not come to her as often as she wanted him.

CHAPTER SEVEN

The following day dawned bright, warmth from the early-morning sun caressing Brandy softly as she pushed aside the glass door to the patio. She had awakened prematurely, thoughts of the confrontation with Brad filtering through her mind in total recall.

Twenty-one days. Three weeks was all the time he would give her. That would be less than three months after the funeral. Such a short time between Daniel's death and Brad's deadline for their marriage. Her friends would be shocked and her godfather horrified that she wanted to remarry so quickly. Not even a decent interval, everyone would exclaim critically. But what is a socially acceptable period of mourning? Six months? A year? Why should one day make it more correct than another?

Brad's words came back to her. His harsh statement that he would find it impossible to seek another woman if she were to die.

True! How true! If—God forbid—Brad should be taken from her, she knew it would be repugnant to contemplate another man possessing her. Perhaps a decent interval is related more to intensity of love or need rather than social custom. Brad's memory would demand an infinity.

Tears brimmed her eyes, but she blinked them away in

an attempt to control her depression. Her life had to go on. Grief could be kept in the forefront, worried over and painful, or relinquished to a proper place in one's memories.

Brandy's life with Daniel had slipped into the past the moment her eyes locked with Brad's in the lounge. The one memorable point in time she admitted her devastating love. Love Brad had taken as totally as he had taken her body.

His anger returned to haunt her while she dressed. She hadn't heard a sound beyond the communicating door, but the rooms were solid, noise not easily perceived. Would he burst into her room and demand she submit? She would be foolish to doubt his intentions. Brad would use her when he desired. His overpowering strength had been proved but would be unnecessary.

One look, a single touch, and she was putty in his hands. Long years of self-denial had built up like a stockpile of fuel. Brad was the torch to ignite it.

"Dear God," she moaned, "I need his loving so terribly much."

She felt a trembling start in the pit of her stomach as she walked to the bathroom to apply makeup. Senses that Brad had brought to burgeoning life now cried out for fulfillment. Remembrance of the lingering caresses of his long tanned fingers smoothing suntan lotion into her body brought a flush of desire. When he stroked the swell of her breasts, she had suppressed the urge to roll onto her back, limbs parting, arms reaching to accept his body.

The intimacy of Brad's searing kiss in the pool brought a bright spot of color to her cheeks as she added a final flick of mascara to her heavy lashes. His body had tightened, his male need rousing as she clung to his wet shoulders. With legs entwined his hips had been thrust slightly forward, one powerful arm pushing against her buttocks as they sank below the water.

With a final spray of cologne settling on her shoulders Brandy shook her head, hoping to end the turmoil of her sudden introspection. Her vibrant chestnut hair raised in a silky cloud before curving back to rest against her nape.

The heck with Brad. She would go to her godfather, enjoy a leisurely breakfast, and take a taxi into town. She refused to be intimidated. If he expected her to cower in a corner like a shy, innocent maiden waiting for her inevitable ravishment, he was very much mistaken. She may be a slave to her own sexual desires but damned if she'd be a slave to his!

With determined strides she walked toward the coffee shop, the short skirt of her amber and navy print dress flowing around her legs. The sharp heels of her sandals made a loud clicking noise on the tiled floor when she entered the sunlit room.

Dismay filled her when she observed Brad seated across from James and the colonel at a table set for four. His short-sleeve knit shirt in dark navy-blue emphasized the width of his shoulders and deep tan of his well-muscled forearms. Her breath caught when he glanced up, a smile of welcome showing his strong white teeth.

He's gorgeous, she thought, walking forward. A gorgeous male animal in the prime of life. Vigorous, masculine, and totally aware of his power over her emotions.

"Welcome, Brandy. Your timing is perfect. I rang your room and, when there was no answer, assumed you were on your way down. We're about to order." His hand touched the naked skin of her arm, bared in her sleveless

123

dress. As he rose to seat her at his side, his fingers surreptitiously caressed her back.

"It's about time!" her godfather grumbled. "I want my cereal. Can't start a day without my oatmeal," he informed them despite their lack of interest. "Not that instant stuff either. They fix it right here. Slow-cooked old-fashioned oats like a man is supposed to eat. Right?"

"Yes, Godfather," Brandy chuckled. "We know you eat oatmeal every morning and a bowl of soup before the start of every dinner."

"Do you good too, child. You're too thin. Right, Brad?"

Brad turned his head, his glance lingering on Brandy's slender arms and the enticing thrust of her mature rounded breasts. "Brandy is slim, Colonel, but not too much so."

Her breast rose and fell with agitation when he continued, his manner, as always, unperturbed by her embarrassment.

"I think her figure is perfect. Absolutely flawless in fact. All that I've seen of course!" Brad added in a droll voice. Which was everything, his look reminded her.

"Too thin," her godfather disagreed. "In my youth we appreciated more meat on a woman's bones. Our women were curvy front and back. Some of those women parading around your pool look like emaciated young boys. Right, James?"

James remained silent, paying little attention to his employer's outburst. He had listened to his opinions with an open mind for years.

Brandy's eyes scanned the menu, deciding coffee and an English muffin would be ample, grimacing as Brad and

James ordered complete breakfasts including ham, eggs, hashed brown potatoes, and toast.

"Bring a large glass of fresh-squeezed orange juice for the young lady, Susan," Brad requested, calling the waitress by her first name.

"I don't want juice, Brad," she insisted, knowing her voice sounded irritated by his assumption that she could not care for herself without his help.

"I don't care if you want it or not, you'll drink it. A pregnant woman needs vitamins and proper nutrition to give birth to a healthy child."

"Of all the nerve . . ." she sputtered.

"Brad's right, Brandy. Do as he says. We want our baby robust, don't we?" the colonel asked, unaware his words were apropos.

"Yes, we most certainly want *our* baby and mother to always be in the best of health," Brad agreed, enjoying Brandy's discomfort as he added fuel to her fiery temper.

Damn him! She fumed silently, lashes lowered to shield the glitter of anger sparking in her eyes. He acts as if he has every right to control my life already. Arrogant beast.

Sipping a cup of hot black coffee, Brandy was forced to admire his composure. Last night's wrath might not have happened. He was courteous and respectful to her and the two men. It seemed impossible that he actually threatened to tell the colonel that he, not Daniel, was the father of her unborn child. She would have sworn on a Bible that Brad would never do a thing to harm the old man . . . yet, each warning was imprinted on her mind!

"More coffee, Brandy?" Brad inquired when their waitress returned with the pot.

"Yes, thank you," she answered quickly, jealousy rushing through her at the inviting smile of the attractive

125

redheaded waitress. The way she tried to press her body against Brad as she leaned across the booth set Brandy's teeth on edge. Made her want to tell her to leave him alone. He was hers . . . totally, irrevocably, hers.

My God, now I'm acting like a jealous fishwife, she thought. *He has destroyed my composure, threatened me, my life is in havoc, yet I ache for a good-morning kiss so much, I can barely sit beside him without reaching over to pull his mouth to mine.*

Brad reached beneath the table, his fingers trailing across her thigh before stopping to rub her knee in slow, lingering strokes. His touch drove her wild.

"Er—what, Godfather?" Brandy asked, not hearing his question.

"I asked you did you know where Brad's taking us today? What's wrong with you, girl? You've acted peculiar ever since we got here."

"Leave her be, Colonel. I hear pregnant women always act strange," Brad teased. "Or perhaps the company of three charming men for an entire day has overwhelmed her."

Her godfather's loud guffaw followed, mingling with James's sympathetic glance. James knew what was wrong. Brandy could tell by his glance he was thinking of Brad's confidences and warning about his intentions to marry her. The news had given him an insight into her sudden confusion and lack of equanimity.

Brandy winced at the pressure of Brad's hand when he gripped her knee covertly. His hand raised to calmly lift his own coffee cup. She watched him sip his drink slowly, knowing he was aware of her discomfort. Undoubtedly enjoying it too, she decided, giving him a veiled glare.

"Brandy, I asked you a question," her godfather reprimanded her. Using rich coffee cream from the pitcher on the table instead of milk that came with his cereal, he glanced sheepishly to see if Brandy noticed.

"Er—what?" Then suddenly she remembered. "No."

"Forgot, did you? I told you the first night here that Brad had plans for each day of our vacation. Today we go for a drive." He sneaked a piece of Brad's hot buttered toast and dunked it in the creamy oatmeal, chewing the soggy end with relish while waiting to hear what Brandy had to say.

"In your Cadillac?" she asked, knowing he always refused to ride in anything else, yet not able to picture Brad allowing another man to drive him around.

"Of course not! Brad's driving us. James and I will sit in the backseat. Be a change for you, huh, James?" he chuckled.

"Yes, sir, Colonel." James smiled, enjoying his inclusion in the day's pleasures.

"Brad showed me his new Lincoln Continental," her godfather told her smugly. "Might get me one when we get home. A man has to keep up with progress, you know."

Oh, my God . . . I can't believe it, she thought. *He's a complete turncoat, the old devil.* She loved him even more because of his unpredictability.

"Well, I don't know where you three will be going today, but I'm going to take a taxi into town and spend the day window-shopping," Brandy announced smugly.

"Not today, you're not," Brad told her calmly. "Last night you felt ill, and I think it best that you relax today. A leisurely drive will benefit you even more than last night's did."

"Godfather!" Brandy looked at him, pleading he put

Brad in his place. After all, to the colonel he was still a relative stranger.

"Listen to Brad, girl. He has your best interests at heart, I'm sure. Right, Brad?"

"Right, Colonel," Brad answered, his short clipped speech warning her to be careful.

Deciding she had had enough, Brandy rose. If she heard one more "Right, Brad?" from her godfather, she would explode.

"Excuse me, please. I want to freshen my makeup." Without a backward glance Brandy stormed from the room, head tilted at a defiant angle. The fury in her threatened to overcome her common sense. Needing a release, adrenaline pumping through her bloodstream at a furious rate, she walked up the two flights of stairs, calling Brad every mean name she could think of.

Entering the suite, she was shocked to see him sitting on the edge of her bed, legs crossed, arm raised as he checked his watch.

"One minute fifty-eight seconds. Pretty good, but the elevator's quicker."

"Damn you, Brad! What are you doing in my room?" Brandy asked, nerves shaking at his audacity.

"Sitting on my bed in my room. You're living in my suite," he reminded her confidently.

"I know that. What do you want with me?"

"You dare ask that leading question knowing I'm filled with frustration from our intermittent love play?"

"Intermittent? You sound like a weather forecast," she sassed, easing around him toward the bathroom, intent on rushing inside and locking the door. Even if she had to stay inside the room all day, it would be worth it to be free of his taunts and mocking face.

Aware of Brandy's intentions, Brad rose, deliberately standing between her and the doorway. As she stepped backward his hand snaked out and grabbed her wrist in a firm hold.

"How's this for a weather report, then? Cool days and hot nights ahead for the next three weeks, plus sensual turbulence with the possibility of hurricane-force sex!"

"Why, you—you—maniac."

"Shut up. The colonel and James are waiting. I came up here to kiss the living hell out of you starting right now."

In one swift motion Brad took her mouth with a harsh groan. His fixity of purpose frightened her, the strength of his arms overpowering as he pulled her upward. Angered that she kept her lips clenched, he slid his hands from her shoulders to her face, fingers cupping the side of her neck, palms steadying her jaw.

Brandy fought his attempt to part her lips, furious that he thought he could use her at will. She struggled vainly, breasts heaving as she wrenched free for a brief moment.

"Arrogant beast!" she exclaimed, her face raised in defiance of him. He towered over her petite height, his tall powerful build intimidating. Damn him! Her thoughts were mirrored in the glittering depths of her uniquely colored eyes. Controlled by his hand on her nape, she stamped her foot in fury.

A smile tugged his lips, the lazy nonchalance of his stance irritating her even further.

"Why didn't you get this horrible punishment over with when you woke this morning?" she blurted out.

"Because, my dear not-so-sweet wife-to-be, I slept at home. As mad as I was over your deception, I knew if I stayed here I'd spend the night giving you several bouts of that 'horrible punishment' that you crave as much as

I do. I preferred making love to you rather than having sex."

"There's a difference?" she questioned sarcastically.

With a jerk he gripped her shoulders, giving her a single shake. "How innocent you really are. What we shared in Las Vegas was love. Every touch was meant to *give* pleasure not take it. The final climax was shared in equal intensity. To have sex with you, my only interest would be to take not give."

"Like now. Seemed the same as always to me!" she snapped.

Hard fingers squeezed her shoulders in punishment, as his breath fanned her mouth with each angry word of warning.

"If you want to know the difference, keep sassing me now or in front of the colonel and James plus flaunting your sexy little butt around like you did when you left the breakfast table in a huff. You'll damn well find out how divergent my needs are with both sex and love too!"

"Horrible monster." Without thought for the possible consequences she turned her face quickly in an attempt to bite his hand.

Brad easily avoided her bite and swooped her up into his arms.

"By God, witch, your first lesson starts right now." His mouth clamped over her lips, smothering her gasp as they sank to the wide bed together.

Pinned beneath his weight, she knew her struggles were useless. His anger fired her blood and ignited a primitive spark of urgency to meet his need with equal wildness. The desire to bite in anger changed to the need to bite his taut flesh in a gesture of intense love.

His tongue invaded her parted lips, but the fierce, angry

thrust turned into slow, deliberate motions with the intent to incite. A ruthless plundering that she reveled in.

Gasping for breath, Brandy clung to him, her body arching to meet his hardened masculinity. She squirmed closer, instinctively knowing each motion that would drive him into a frenzy of frustration.

Brad's mouth left her parted lips to nibble a path along her neck, easily slipping the narrow straps of her sleeveless top aside.

"Hmm . . . such beautiful shoulders," he muttered, his voice filled with torment. His tongue flicked over her smooth skin on the swell of her breasts along the scalloped edge of her bra.

His eyes lingered longingly on her heaving breasts as she lay beneath him, her hips suddenly stopping their instinctive languorous undulations. With shaky fingers he pulled the skimpy bra below her full breasts. Her nipples were erect, tantalizing buds awaiting his lips. A moan came from deep in his body as he took one, then the other, into his mouth. His firm tongue flicked over them erotically before he teased her with delicate nips from his strong teeth.

Brandy clung to his shoulders, soft whimpers of excitement coming from her quivering lips. Totally overcome by Brad's mastery of her senses, she clasped him to her breast, wanting the new sensual foreplay to go on and on. Her stomach muscles clenched convulsively; her limbs trembled.

Brad raised his weight from her, his eyes darkened with lust as they ran over the beauty of her face flushed with passion from his touch. They lingered on her full breasts while he pulled the cups back over the sensitive tips.

"You have one of those sexy bras on again. Designed by

a man, no doubt, just to drive another man wild. Do you have on matching panties too?"

Brandy flushed at his blatant words. Squirming to get away from his hips that pinned her to the soft mattress, she thought of the other men she had known. None of them would have dreamed of speaking his mind like Brad. From their first coming together in Las Vegas Brad was blunt in his speech. He had told her exactly what he wanted, been eager to let her know how she pleased him, and as open in his request that she tell him what she liked.

"You'll darn well not find out."

Husky laughter filled the room while he eased his large frame from her. Standing beside the tumbled bed, he stared at her, his smile indulgent.

"Prim little miss all of a sudden, aren't you?" his voice teased. "I'll be good and let my imagination run riot all day long. My thoughts are filled with the taste of you now. It will add a little sensual excitement to the day."

Brandy pulled the straps of her dress over her shoulders. Gracefully she climbed off the opposite side of the bed, intent on reaching the bathroom to repair the damage to her makeup.

Brad watched with amusement, delighted by the look of her with her bright brunette hair a tangled mass of silken waves. He relaxed, settling comfortably into a bedside chair thinking of the next three weeks with eager anticipation.

In a few minutes Brandy returned, hair smoothed, dress straightened, and makeup impeccably applied. The slight flush, full quivering lips, and dilated pupils were a giveaway that she had been as aroused as Brad.

A confident smile touched his face, his voice soft and serious.

"Get your longest gold chain."

"Why?"

"Get it and you'll see."

With a shrug she walked to the dresser and removed a narrow necklace from her jewelry case before returning to Brad with a quizzical look on her face.

"Give it to me." Easing his broad frame from the chair, he reached into his slacks pocket, retracting a small object.

Brandy watched with dawning dismay as he unclasped her chain and slipped a wide gold band over it. With deft fingers he refastened the clasp carefully before meeting her look. His eyes narrowed to partially conceal his serious mood as he walked forward. Speechless, Brandy stood on trembling legs while he lowered the chain over her head.

With a reverent touch he placed his ring in the deep cleavage between her breasts. He smoothed her hair neatly around her neck, looking at her for a moment before drawing her into his arms. His mouth took hers in a gentle kiss, then he hugged her to his broad chest. God, he wanted her!

She could feel the rapid beating of his heart, the trembling of his hands against her back, before a soft husky murmur escaped his lips. His chin rested on her hair while he explained his need to give her a symbol of love.

"Wear it there for the next twenty days."

Brandy slipped from his hold, stunned by his sudden tenderness. "I can't wear it. We're not married."

"We are a hell of a lot more married than you and Daniel were. God, but I hate that name even." Brad, now agitated, paced the floor, his hand rubbing his neck in contemplation before he burst out grimly, "All those years without making love to you. Was he crazy? How could any man keep his hands off you for five minutes much less five years?"

Tears brimmed her eyes at Brad's careless words. She shook her head to refute his statement but he continued bitterly.

"No, I guess he wasn't crazy. The colonel tells me his son was a brilliant attorney, an excellent student, but not —at his sorrow—a military man." Brad stopped, pinning her with a hard fierce look, his jealousy barely concealed. "Tell me about Daniel now, Brandy. Tell me!"

Brandy shook her head, adamantly refusing his demand. She held back tears with practiced composure, her voice firm and convincing.

"No, Brad. I will tell you nothing of my marriage."

Brad stared at her; he was filled with disgust that he would not hear the reasons behind her platonic marriage but forced to admire her refusal to relate the slightest detail.

Checking his watch, he groaned before clasping her elbow and guiding her to the door. "We've been up here forty-five minutes. The colonel and James will wonder what the hell is happening."

They walked to the elevator, the short ride over in seconds before striding into the foyer where the colonel waited impatiently. James stood beside him, observing Brandy's face without comment.

"Good thing you have comfortable chairs, Brad. I was getting tired of waiting. Told James to go get you, but he wouldn't do it. Thought I needed looking after, I guess." The colonel stood up, his stride brisk as they walked four abreast through the open glass doors to Brad's waiting car.

"What was the problem anyway?" he asked curiously

before easing into the backseat of the comfortable Lincoln Continental

"Brandy, you sit up front," Brad commanded, gripping her elbow when she tried to follow her godfather into the rear seat. After they were seated, Brad pulled from the long drive before answering the colonel's question.

"I went to get Brandy and she looked pale and distraught. I insisted she lay on her bed for a short rest."

"Well, she looks rested now to me, though her face is a little flushed." The colonel leaned forward, placing his hand on Brandy's shoulder lovingly. "Are you okay, child? No problems with our baby, is there?"

Brad gave her a veiled glance when she looked over her shoulder to reply.

"No, Godfather. We—we're both fine."

"Might be a good idea to start your prenatal care here in Palm Springs. Right, Brad?"

"Brad? What does Brad have to do with my pregnancy?" she blurted out unthinkingly before lowering her lashes to conceal her oversight.

She clasped her fingers nervously around the capacious purse in her lap. *My God! What does Brad have to do with it? Only everything. Without him there would be no pregnancy.*

Brad tensed, biting back his inclination to tell the colonel he was the baby's father not Daniel. He was anxious to claim his unborn child. His possessive personality and attitude of proprietorship toward Brandy and their baby was driving him mad to remain silent. Twenty days and the world would know. Less than three weeks and Brandy would also be his legally. She had been his physically for over a month. His claim had been made in Nevada and was irrevocable.

"Settle down, Brandy," the colonel reprimanded gruffly, breaking into their deep introspection. "Brad will know a competent gynecologist."

Laughter filled the car as Brandy giggled, her natural sense of humor coming to the fore. "Now I've heard of everything, Godfather. Brad would be the last person to need the services of a gynecologist." Her eyes sparkled with amusement as they lingered on Brad's broad masculine frame. His arms were muscled, thighs lithe yet fitting his size. If anyone in the world was the epitome of overt masculinity, it was Brad.

Displeased by his goddaughter's laughter, the colonel scolded, his short hair bristling as he leaned over to tap her shoulder sharply.

"Hold your tongue, child. This is serious business. You need vitamins and a checkup."

"What did your doctor in Pasadena say, Brandy?" Brad asked without embarrassment, uncaring that he would normally have no interest in a stranger's pregnancy.

"She hasn't seen one yet," the colonel butted in. "Darn fool thing too, seeing how important this baby is to all of us."

"You mean Brandy's pregnancy hasn't even been confirmed?" Brad asked harshly, his jaw taut, eyes shifting to Brandy.

"No. She told me that being as she's had one child already, she knew as much as the doctor did." The colonel guffawed loudly, looking to see if the others were enjoying his banter. "One baby and she thinks she's got more knowledge than someone with eight or so years of medical school."

"Godfather, please be quiet!" Brandy scolded abruptly,

becoming increasingly irritated with their carrying on a conversation about her as if she weren't there.

Dismayed by the news that Brandy had not had a positive pregnancy check and was going on assumption, Brad stared at her, his look warning her to be still. *Many more surprises about her from the colonel and I'll have an ulcer,* he reasoned. That she had deceived her godfather, argued, and refused to confide in him plagued him constantly. He ached to know everything now and yet was forced to wait, getting piece by changing piece, one little portion at a time.

"I'll make an appointment in the morning, Colonel. Now if you'll look ahead to the right, you will see the start of *TV Guide* publisher Walter C. Annenberg's vast estate with its acres of landscaped grounds, trees, lakes, golf course, and luxurious buildings. From the air it is even more impressive, since it contrasts so vividly with the surrounding desert."

Everyone agreed with Brad, enjoying the opportunity of being escorted around the area by a longtime resident. Brad was an excellent raconteur, telling them amusing stories as he drove. His knowledge emcompassed everything about the area; he even readily identified the unique flora and fauna native to the Coachella Valley Desert. The colonel and James were delighted, listening attentively to each word.

Brandy had been tense, fearful that the day would be difficult. To her amazement Brad couldn't have been more considerate. He was careful to watch that the colonel didn't become too tired and was equally attentive to James.

Returning to Casa del Oro after an excellent meal at the

Lord Fletcher Inn, Brad escorted the colonel and James to their room for a brief visit prior to their afternoon naps.

Brandy had received a casual nod when they parted company in the broad foyer. Miffed by his indifference, she stormed to her room, forced to admit she was even jealous over the undivided attention he had given James and the colonel throughout the day.

She tried the door handle to Brad's suite, hoping to look through it while he was busy. It was latched securely. Thwarted by her attempt to snoop, she went into the bathroom and took a long cold shower, which did nothing to dampen her temper.

Within moments she had applied makeup, dressed in a short-sleeve teal-blue dress with white banding on the hem and neckline, slipped into sandals, grabbed her purse, and was seated in a taxi, traveling toward the downtown shopping area.

As she walked into one store after another her packages increased alarmingly. She looked at the latest one-piece bathing suits with their deep plunging necklines and indecently high-cut bottoms, debated briefly, then purchased a vivid green jersey bikini equally revealing. It enhanced her petite curved figure with flattering perfection, and she hoped Brad would be shocked when he first saw her wearing it. Dresses followed, cool gowns, strappy sandals, and capacious handbags in outrageous colors. All were expensive but no more so than at the finer stores in Pasadena. Feeling better, she returned to the resort.

Disappointed that Brad didn't observe her grand entrance followed by the smitten cab driver with his arms full of bags and boxes, she went to her suite. She placed everything in drawers or on hangers before meeting the colonel for dinner dressed in one of her colorful new dresses. The evening was long and filled with frustration as she talked with her godfather alone. Brad did not appear, nor did her subtle hints about his whereabouts bring forth any comment. A miserable evening followed when she realized she would not hear from Brad and that his suite next door was empty.

More days followed along the same pattern, while the weather stayed glorious. Each was filled with balmy warmth and clear blue skies. Brad met them every morning for breakfast, telling them of his plans for the day and checking to see that the colonel wasn't too tired.

They visited Palm Canyon, run by the Agua Caliente Indians, and viewed its beautiful stand of native Washingtonia palms estimated to be nearly two thousand years old. Their walk through the four acres of the Botanical Gardens on Palm Canyon Drive, containing over two thousand varieties of desert plants from all over the world, took up another morning. The plants were rare, with interesting shapes and blooms.

The colonel received permission from his doctor to ride on the Palm Springs Aerial Tramway. Traveling in the hanging trams for the two-and-a-half-mile span from the desert valley floor to the verdant forest mountaintop was unforgettable. Ascending the eighty-five hundred feet to the top, they climbed through eight different climate zones. The spectacular view of the rugged San Jacinto Mountains was awe inspiring. Brad had brought a picnic lunch, which they consumed hungrily while basking in the invigorating change of scenery. The heady scent of pine woods filled their nostrils with its pungent odor, adding to their pleasure. Chattering jays and chipmunks begging for food amused them all.

On another day Brad took them to the Living Desert

Reserve in Palm Desert. Devoted to the preservation of native plants and animals, it contained the largest captive herd of bighorn sheep in the United States on its thousand acres of land. The colonel was unable to walk along its footpaths but enjoyed the exhibits with all the enthusiasm of the numerous children crowded around him.

Returning from the reserve, Brad looked at Brandy.

"Too bad you didn't come here last month. We hold our annual rodeo in February and the entire town gets involved. Shorts and casual shirts are replaced by tight jeans, boots, stetsons, and western shirts."

Before Brandy could speak up, the colonel broke in. "We'd have liked that. Right, James? We never miss a cowboy movie on TV if we can help it."

"How about you, Brandy? Do you like cowboys too?" Brad asked, deliberately eliminating movies from his question.

Pleased by his sudden attention, she smiled, her eyes velvety soft with humor. "Don't know, since I've never met any. Marina del Rey and Pasadena are both short on real cowboys."

"Well, I'll have to introduce you to some when we travel to Flagstaff, Arizona, this summer. The colonel and James have already accepted my invitation for a few weeks vacation. I have another smaller resort there. More rustic, with a few less amenities, but the plumbing is indoors," he teased.

Brandy looked over her shoulder at her godfather's smug expression, thinking that Brad had taken over their lives and there didn't appear to be one thing they could do about it even if they objected. His strength of purpose was more apparent each day.

"Wait till you see the brochure on it. James and I may never go home now. Right, James? Right, Brad?" her godfather told her.

Brad's deep laughter caused his broad shoulders to rise and fall as he eased into the Casa del Oro parking lot space reserved for his big Lincoln Continental. Brandy's heart lurched just watching him.

"You and James look and feel so much better since taking your daily mineral baths, it would be a shame to let your deep tans fade by leaving us," Brad added sincerely.

Brad again escorted the colonel and James to their rooms, giving Brandy an amused smile as if perfectly aware of her ill mood. "We will go to Indio tomorrow, Brandy. Be ready at nine."

"I may," she hissed beneath her breath so only Brad could hear. "Then again I may not." She knew full well she wouldn't miss it.

"Nine o'clock, witch, or I'll come get you," he warned bluntly.

Ready at nine sharp, Brandy enjoyed the loop to the city of Indio. Brad showed them producing date farms, explaining the complicated care needed for the towering palms. They had also missed the annual February Riverside County Date Festival with its unique expositions plus camel and ostrich races. They drank thick, creamy date malts, a delicious treat that the colonel relished, grumbling beneath his breath when advised that two might make him ill.

Several evenings the four of them ate leisurely dinners together. Brad escorted them to the finest restaurants in town despite the fact that his own surpassed them all. He acted determined to see that the colonel and James were never bored. Everywhere they went he was greeted with respect and admiration from the men and obvious attention from the numerous beautiful women. They dined at the Hungry Tiger, the cozy Smoke Tree Lounge overlooking the pool, the Agua Room of the Spa with its excellent cuisine, the Tropics Steakhouse, the Octillo Room, and the gourmet dining room at the Sheraton Plaza, which was just opening for its first season.

After dinner Brad would visit with the two men briefly, then leave. Several nights he stayed away completely. Jealousy ate at Brandy's peace of mind as she pictured him kissing another woman before taking her to his bed. *For all I know, he might have a dozen mistresses in town,* she mused.

During their meals together Brad made certain his leg never touched Brandy's, nor did his hand slip beneath the table to linger on her thigh or clasp her knee. She was treated impersonally, causing her agitation to mount daily at an alarming pace.

On the fourteenth day she stormed to her room in disgust, impolitely leaving their dinner table without an apology or single explanation to anyone. Her hands clenched into tight fists after slamming the door shut. She grumbled aloud, sounding as irritable as her godfather, her eloquent voice echoing in the empty suite.

"Damn you, Mr. Brad Lucas! You are an arrogant beast. First you scare me to death with your sensual ultimatums and then you don't even make one single attempt to force me to submit to . . . anything!"

Pacing back and forth across the floor in nervous agitation, Brandy exclaimed with a bitter laugh, "Submit? My

142

gosh, I'm so lonesome for your attention, I feel like propositioning you myself," she exclaimed, pacing nervously across the floor.

She removed her clothes, carelessly dropping them on the foot of the bed before walking to the bathroom. A long period of time soaking in her most expensive bath salts did nothing to soothe her nerves. With brisk strokes she dried her wet limbs before applying an excess of powder, uncaring that it left a layer of white on the bathroom carpet around her feet.

Clad in her favorite pair of gold Chinese-style pajamas, she turned on the television and raised the sound to blot out her own verbal complaints. Brushing her hair viciously, she sat cross-legged in the middle of the king-size bed, venting her fury with each stroke.

"If your ring wasn't nestling between my breasts, Brad Lucas, I wouldn't believe you even noticed I was staying here!" Her angry voice mingled with that of Joan Fontaine in *Born to Be Bad* as she indifferently watched the glossy soap-opera-type movie.

Laying her brush down, she reached for the telephone to dial the coffee shop.

"This is Ms. Harcourt. Would you happen to have any popcorn? Yes, I said popcorn. I would like the candied type like Screaming Yellow Zonkers. Good, send me a box, please."

Satisfied, Brandy waited, knowing her sudden craving for something sweet would be placated. Within minutes a waiter arrived with her order, smiling at the unusual late-night snack. Searching through the basket of fruit, kept fresh each day, Brandy found a large red Washington Delicious apple.

Propped against the headboard, she watched television avidly . . . between bites of crisp juicy apple and sweet glazed popcorn. She watched one movie after another, unable to sleep, ending with a scary thriller by Alfred Hitchcock.

CHAPTER EIGHT

Brad entered through the communicating door into Brandy's room. It was five o'clock in the morning and still pitch-black outside, but the light from his room shone bright. A steady hum from the television set resounded through the room, the blank screen attesting to the early hour. His eyes took in the disorder, an indulgent smile crossing his face as he glanced toward her before turning off the TV.

Brandy, curled in the middle of the bed, lay in a small heap. Her glistening dark hair spilled on the pillow in tangled disarray. Brad set his packages down and walked to the side of the bed. He watched for long moments before kneeling on the bed to wake her.

"Wake up, sleepyhead," he whispered against her face.

A sleepy mumble was Brandy's only reaction. Curled on her side, facing Brad, she remained still.

A featherlight kiss was placed across her cheek to no avail. Brad's weight pulled against the sheet but that didn't cause any noticeable effect either. Impatient after the two weeks without touching her, he stretched along the spread, his mouth seeking her lips.

Brandy awoke with a start when he touched her mouth, a high-pitched scream stifled by Brad's mouth closing over hers in a passionate greeting. She knew instantly who it was and raised her arms to bring his beloved face closer.

Deep murmurs of satisfaction came from both their throats as the tender kiss lengthened.

Brad smiled, pleased by her escalating response and that she awoke with an innate willingness to receive his affection. When tears spilled from her eyes and touched his cheek, he drew away, leaning on the edge of the bed to watch.

"Why are you here, Brad?" she questioned, sitting up with a groan. A piercing headache brought a frown, and she rubbed her forehead.

"Headache, honey?" Brad asked with concern. She looked so sensual, with her tumbled hair and innocent face flushed with sleep. He sighed with regret, wanting to take her desperately.

"A terrible one."

"Lack of sleep?"

"Probably."

"You must have had quite a night. Your room looks like a pigpen. What did you do, woman?"

Expression impudent, she quipped smartly, "You tell me!"

"Let me see how good a detective I am, then," Brad told her, bending forward to prowl around the room in an exaggerated spoof of Sherlock Holmes, peering right and left.

Brandy's elated laughter brought a shining beauty to her widened eyes. She drew her knees up, watching with rapt expression as Brad spoke.

"Hmm . . . I see one female, in her twenties, who indulged in an angry temper tantrum, stomping out of the dining room."

"Cheater," she retorted. "You knew that. Tell me something you didn't see."

"Hush, witch. This same messy young woman removed her clothes sloppily," he stated, noticing her rumpled dress and underwear on the foot of the bed, "took a bath" —Brad returned from a brief foray into the bathroom— "and used bath salts and powder in excess. She dried her hair in the bedroom," he continued, spotting the wrinkled towel on the rug beside the bed with her hairbrush on top, "but it's not too clear now what she did."

Brad put his fingertips to his forehead, brows drawn together in serious contemplation, while Brandy watched, entranced.

"Ah, yes, Doctor Watson, I get the picture now. This same slovenly female went to bed and indulged in a veritable orgy of decadent bliss!"

Brandy followed Brad's eyes while he listed each thing she had done, barely able to suppress a series of childlike giggles.

"Apparently part of the coddling was an apple." He held up the withered core resting in the bedside ashtray. "Drank a glass of Perrier water." He looked at the empty green bottle. "Expensive tastes, I'm afraid. And ate an entire box of an unidentified substance." Brad picked up the box and looked inside quizzically. "What the hell is this stuff?"

"You're the detective, Sherlock," she teased, "so figure it out yourself." Pleased with Brad's attention, Brandy delighted in his silly mood.

He held the box in front of his face, hand over his eyes. "It's coming to me!" he mocked, peeking through his spread fingers. "Yes, I get it now. It's clearly a box of

Screaming Yellow Zonkers—my God, what a name—which are a sweet glazed crispy light popcorn snack."

"Did I miss anything?"

"You tell me."

"Ah, yes." Spotting the *TV Guide,* he added, "The suspect watched one of three things: one: a program; two: a test pattern; three: a program and fell asleep, missing the test pattern entirely!"

"You're insane, Brad."

"Insane heck. I'm brilliant. Am I right?"

"Almost."

"What did I miss?"

"The name of the movie I watched!" she sassed impudently.

Brad threw his hands out in exasperation and teased mischievously, "Sherlock Holmes and Dr. Watson didn't reveal all their clues."

He reached across the wide bed and dragged Brandy from the covers until she stood before him, feet bare and arms clinging to his waist.

Her face rested against Brad's chest, his height even more formidable with his feet in boots. Inhaling the clean smell of his cotton shirt and feeling his body's warmth seep through to her face and hands caused her to sigh with contentment.

"Well, woman . . . tell me. What did you watch?" His hands clasped behind her back, keeping her tight against his body.

Brandy pushed against him, her hands slipping between them to play with the shiny snaps on his shirt. "Actually the last thing I remember clearly was being in a frenzy of terror watching *Frenzy.*"

Brad's chest rose and fell, his hands unclasping to slide up and down Brandy's spine over her pajama top.

"Hmm . . . I like these silky pj's. Almost as sleek as your skin." One large hand slipped beneath her pajama top, over her rib cage, to cup her naked breast. A shudder passed through his palm into her body when he moaned.

"God, no, it's not. No material in the world feels like the texture of your satiny breasts." His thumb caressed her nipple into an erect peak before reluctantly pulling away.

Brad clasped her neck, raising her chin with his thumb. He placed a hungry kiss on her parted lips, but suddenly lifted his head and, scowling, pushed her toward the bathroom with a light swat on her firm buttocks.

"Get dressed, woman! We're going horseback riding."

"Is it safe? I don't have anything to wear anyway," she explained, taking clean underwear from her dresser, unaware her naked curves were outlined beneath the thin silk pajamas.

"I talked with a doctor. There will be no problem if we walk or canter our horses gently since you are an experienced equestrienne. Take those packages." He pointed to the table as he turned on a lamp to brighten the room. "Everything is in there."

Brandy stared at Brad as he walked to the communicating door and closed it firmly. He had thought of the possibility that she didn't bring riding clothes with her, so he purchased them without saying a word or asking her sizes.

She stopped in the doorway to the bathroom, head tilted while giving him a thorough once-over.

His clothes were casual, enhancing his masculinity. From the tips of his heavy leather cowboy boots, tight-legged brown western jeans, western belt with silver buckle, to the skin-hugging western shirt in deep burgundy, he caused her heartbeat to increase. He wore no hat and she suspected he would find it unnecessary. His hair was thick and always lay in unfettered waves, ruggedly handsome.

"Quit giving me the eye and get dressed. I'm rushing you out this door in fifteen minutes."

With the packages under her arm Brandy shot into the bathroom. Her fingers fumbled in her haste to dress quickly, but she managed to return to the living area in ten minutes.

Brad's eyes narrowed as he looked at her bright happy face. It was the first time he had seen her dressed in slacks and she was beautiful. A tiny perfection of femininity.

Each item fit her petite figure as if custom sewn. The brown designer jeans clung to her legs and hugged her narrow waist. Her blouse was burgundy like his, outlining the swell of her breasts and clinging to her rib cage. Boots and matching belt were polished a deep brown in soft carved leather.

"Do I look okay?" she teased, twirling around to parade before him.

"Brandy, you know damn well you look gorgeous. Those skintight pants hug your derrriere like I want to. Same goes for the blouse. Grab your bathing suit and purse and let's go."

"But what about the colonel and James?"

"They know I'm taking you away for the day. Your godfather needs a day of rest, and besides, I want you to myself."

After Brandy put extra makeup in her purse and checked for tissues and her hairbrush, Brad reached for her elbow, tugging her through the opened doorway and out into the hall. It was still dark, the rooms were quiet, and soft lights filled the hall. They took the elevator to the foyer and walked through the empty office into the cool morning air.

Brandy inhaled the brisk air as Brad helped her into the passenger seat. He was impatient to get to the stables. In less than an hour the sun would rise and he wanted to be far out in the desert, away from man's invasion of nature.

Brandy was silent, her expression rapt, when they arrived at Brad's stables, a short distance from his hotel. They were designed in the same Spanish style, with well-lit landscaped grounds leading to the manager's office.

The fresh tangy smell of horse and clean alfalfa hay reached her nose. She rushed to Brad's side, gripping his arm while smiling with delight. "It's been a long time since I've ridden. I've missed it too! Half my teens were spent on top my huge hunter, either bareback or English. I presume you ride western here?"

"Correct." Brad held her by the waist as his stable foreman came from the rear of the stalls leading two horses. They were saddled, bridled, and appeared eager to exercise their legs across the desert sands.

Brandy watched silently, sizing them up while Brad checked that the cinches were tight. One horse was a deep-muscled gelding with a shiny chestnut coat near the color of her hair. It was saddled with a heavy well-worn man's saddle, and she knew it was Brad's horse. The horse reached its soft muzzle forward to nudge against Brad's chest, giving a short nicker.

Brad affectionately smoothed his hand down the satiny neck and spoke to the horse in a low soothing voice. It responded to his words by flicking its ears back and forth and raising and lowering its head with impatience. Brandy

151

watched the brief interplay with interest, love overflowing her heart that Brad shared her liking for horses.

Holding the reins of the smaller horse, Brad turned to assist Brandy into the saddle. Brandy was standing in front of the dappled gray mare with the silver mane and tail, talking baby talk to it. She placed a kiss on its muzzle, loving the large black eyes and dainty head, unaware of Brad's smile.

"She's beautiful, Brad. What's her name?" Brandy inquired, letting him boost her into the saddle. Settling her feet comfortably into the stirrups, she gathered the reins in her left hand, scooted her buttocks into the padded leather seat, and looked at Brad mischievously, before chiding "Let's go, slowpoke. What's keeping you?"

"Impudent brat," Brad grumbled before swinging into his saddle with a bound, not bothering to use the stirrups. He looked beautiful on top the heavy muscled animal, as if they were a team, one an extension of the other.

They left the stables, their horses shod hooves clomping loud on the paved entrance. Rested, their morning hay and oats consumed, the horses were ready to run. They chomped eagerly at the bits and arched their necks, but they were so well trained, they didn't pull or break out of a swift ground-eating walk.

Brandy looked across her mare's neck, able to see its head move up and down with each stride. The ears were small and well shaped, pricked forward as its attention was on the trail before it. The silky mane lay neatly on one side, white and black hairs intermingling to form a light silver.

"You didn't tell me their names yet, Brad."

"Mine is Whoa Boy. Seriously," he laughed, hearing her snort of disbelief. "Yours is Gray Witch."

"Those are awful names. Why did you pick them?"

"Mine wouldn't stop for the first three years of his life, and yours was a witch until I bred her. One colt settled her right down and she has been a docile little lady ever since."

"I don't believe that."

Ignoring her reply, he turned toward her. "Think it will work with you?"

"Don't count on it!" Brandy retorted indignantly.

The trail took them from the city outskirts right into the barren desert. The sky was rapidly turning a slate-gray. The horses were familiar with the area, having no problem picking their way around the native brush.

"Care to canter?"

Without replying, Brandy clicked her tongue, put her heels to the mare, and leaned forward. The agile quarter horse made one leap and settled into a rolling canter.

Brad held his gelding back and they loped side by side across the sand. The smell of sagebrush was sharp in the brisk air. The dull thudding hoofbeats, the squeak of the leather saddles, and the jangle of bits and bridle chains intermingled. With the cool breeze brushing her face she felt exalted.

They headed for a high knoll. Coming to the wide top, they stopped and let their horses relax. Brad helped her down, his hands lingering on her waist as she slid from the saddle. Nervously brushing back a tumbled curl, she thanked him.

The horses stood quietly, a rear leg cocked at the ankle as they relaxed. The reins hung to the ground. Trained not to move, they would stand for hours ground-tied.

"Do you feel okay?" Brad inquired solicitously.

"I'm hungry."

153

"I didn't mean that."

She laughed up at him, her eyes bright, hair tumbled about her shoulders, and lips parted in a wide smile. "I know it. But I am hungry and I am fine. My headache's gone too!"

Brad led her to a secluded spot, dismounted, checked to make certain it was free of snakes and harmful vermin, then sat down, pulling her with him. They had an unobstructed view of the desert floor.

With his arm around her they sat side by side, neither speaking as the sky turned pink with the dawning of a new day. The sun was a bright circle of crimson as it rose across the horizon, with only a promise of the heat to come.

Still silent, Brad turned her into his arms, his mouth seeking hers in a kiss so tender, expressing such reverence and concern, that tears slipped unbidden from her eyes— tears of happiness that he was no longer filled with anger over her deception.

Brandy sighed, her lips parting as his tongue searched hers to tantalize with languorous strokes. She clasped his nape as they lay down on the cool desert sand. It formed a soft bed beneath her back as Brad pressed against her, one leg moving between hers as she arched upward.

The quiet seduction of his first kiss was forgotten when his passion deepened. Brandy whimpered, moving her hips against him, her hands reaching for the snaps on his shirt, which were easily undone. She ran her fingers across the hard muscles of his chest. She had dreamed many times of freely touching his body since that first night in Las Vegas. Brad had calmly coaxed her into allowing her fervent sensuality to guide her then.

Remembering his heightened desire when she stroked

him, she rubbed back and forth, her fingers tangling in the thick hair.

Brad's mouth left her lips, traveling down her throat to linger on the rapidly beating pulse before moving up to her ear. His incoherent words of affection were whispered over and over as his tongue probed her inner ear. This seductive intimacy never failed to inflame her senses.

Offering no resistance, she allowed him to unsnap her blouse, his mouth sliding over her heaving breasts to rest on the deep cleavage cradling his wedding ring.

"God, Brandy, I could eat you! Your mouth, your breasts, all of you." Brad hovered over her, his eyes filled with desire smoldering like flames in their depths. He bent to kiss her throat, feeling her pulse beat against his lips.

"I ache for you so damn bad, I've wanted you so much lately that I feel like I've been in pain all my life."

Brandy felt her pulses race at his words, felt helpless beneath the urgency of his hands caressing each curve of her body. She lay back, responsive to each caress.

Brad's body was hard against her, his breath raspy as he exhaled against her heaving breasts. His mouth left the enticement of her firm curves and traveled a lingering path to claim once more the sweetness of her parted lips.

His kiss was eternity, making her oblivious of everything around her. Her eyes grew soft, letting him see the love she felt; she was unashamed that her need was equal to his.

Whipcord muscles were taut as steel beneath her fingers as she clung to his shoulders, her nails digging unconsciously in her desire to become one.

"Love me, Brad. Love me here on the desert. Let me be one with you again." Her words spilled forth without

155

thought; she wanted only a repeat of the ecstasy that he had given her within hours of their first meeting.

Brandy's words cooled Brad instantly. He lifted his body from her, drawing her up with him, and balanced her until her legs stopped trembling.

"Time to go back."

A faint flush stained Brandy's cheeks when she raised her face in query.

"I—I thought you wanted me, Brad."

"You know I do!" His fingers felt warm on her breasts as he shakily snapped her blouse. He took her arm and led her back to the horses, who waited patiently on the knoll overlooking the desert below.

"Why didn't you?" she asked, baffled by his sudden coolness.

"No more questions, Brandy. It's time to ride back to the stables." He placed the mare's reins on each side of its neck and, holding them together over its withers, boosted Brandy into the saddle.

It was full daylight now and the heat was rising as rapidly as the sun. Within an hour it would be uncomfortable to ride. The horses' ears pricked up and their strides lengthened when they turned toward the stable. They were as eager to return as they had been to leave.

"Let's canter halfway home," Brad suggested. "That will leave us plenty of time to cool them off before we put them in their stalls."

Brandy dug her heels into the mare's side to canter ahead of Brad's big gelding. Her back was straight and her seat firm as she rode across the sand. Deciding she had gone far enough, she pulled the mare to a stop and spun it around to face Brad.

"She's beautiful, Brad. So responsive to each of my

cues. I think I prefer western to English now. My big hunter could never have spun in the tight circle this little beauty just did."

Brad was amazed at Brandy's ability to control the mare. Her hands were featherlight on the reins, her seat firm in the saddle, showing inherent natural balance.

"She's yours, Brandy."

"You are actually giving me your gray mare?" Brandy exclaimed, her eyes wide with delight.

"I think it appropriate somehow that my little amber-eyed witch become the new owner of Gray Witch. Both of you have given me an alternate mixture of pleasure and pain."

"Thank you, Brad. But we must go to town and get her some carrots and—"

"For God's sake, Brandy," he scolded, bringing his gelding alongside her. "They have the best alfalfa money can buy, oats, sweet feed, and vitamins. They can certainly get by without carrots!"

"Apples, then?" she teased, laughing at his look of consternation.

"Come on, Whoa Boy, let's trot to the stables. Next thing you know she'll want you to wear Italian shoes, designer saddle blankets, and Cartier headstalls."

Brandy laughed as Brad trotted ahead, leaving her to follow at a more sedate pace. He had dismounted and unsaddled and rubbed down Whoa Boy by the time Brandy walked her mare into the stable area.

Before she had time to slip from the saddle, he was there, his hands once again circling her waist to assist her. A stableboy took her mare while Brandy stood motionless, suddenly feeling aches begin in her hips and legs. She hadn't ridden for years and felt every one of her muscles

157

as she walked stiffly to Brad's car. His laughter echoed in her ears; he was aware of her discomfort but knew she would never admit the cause.

Brad eased the Lincoln Continental out of the stable parking lot and drove back toward town. Instead of turning toward the resort, he continued past, through the main section of the city and into the winding drive toward his house.

"No questions?" Brad asked.

"No. I know you well enough by now to know if you intend to take me to your home then nothing I could say or do could change your mind."

"Well, I'll be darned. You're finally learning."

"Actually I'm too hungry to fight and too happy to argue. I feel hot and sticky and anxious to get into something cooler. Today promises to be a scorcher."

"I'll fix you up in a jiff on both counts when we get home. My housekeeper's off today so you'll have to wait while I fix our breakfast."

"As long as I can wait on something more padded than I am, that's fine," she laughed, moving her hips to get comfortable.

"My bed meets those requirements."

"Hmm . . . think of something else."

"My guest-room bed."

"Better, but still too dangerous."

"I thrive on danger," Brad teased, stopping long enough to open the electric gates before driving on to the house.

Brandy looked around, amazed how different everything looked in the daytime. His home was larger than she remembered, sprawling across the hilltop in isolated splendor. Thick adobe walls of natural beige blended with

158

the brown tiled roof. Wide overhanging eaves shaded the numerous windows, keeping out the fierce rays of the noonday sun. Black wrought-iron in intricate patterns was used extensively for decoration and security.

Unique gardens with desert plants and towering palm trees surrounded the brick paths that wound around the landscaped property. Behind the house were a four-car garage and two separate homes secluded from the main residence by an adobe wall.

"Are those the servant quarters?" Brandy asked, pointing to the back area.

Brad stopped in the shade of the patio roof. "One is. My housekeeper and her husband, who takes care of the outside, live there. The bigger house is a separate guest home. I do a lot of entertaining, but I still want my privacy."

"Everything here is such a contrast to my life. My godfather's home is a huge rambling wood-frame structure, while Daniel and I lived on the seventh floor of an ultra modern condominium at the beach."

At the mention of Daniel's name Brad's mouth thinned and he opened the car door with a rough gesture. Heat filled the car like a warm blanket. Air conditioning made it easy to forget they were in the desert with its contrasting climate of cold nights and hot days.

Ignoring his sudden anger, Brandy fanned her face. "Whew, it's warm. We should have gone to your hotel. A cooling swim sounds heavenly." Brandy grimaced when she felt a slight stiffness lingering in her legs.

"Which do you want? Breakfast or a swim first?"

"You have a pool? I don't see it."

"It's around back, hidden by a tall adobe wall. Occasionally we have high winds sweep down sand and grit

159

from the canyons, so we need a wind break. Plus I desire total privacy when I swim."

"That's why you're tan all over," Brandy blurted out without thought, flushing when she noticed his amused smile.

"You will also be tanned . . . all over," Brad warned dryly. "There is a smaller pool out back for my employees and anyone staying in the guest house."

Brandy entered the kitchen ahead of Brad, glancing over the modern kitchen with interest. A sudden urge to cook for Brad overcame her: the age-old desire of the female to provide sustenance for her mate. *He is,* she thought with sudden insight. *Brad is my mate for life.* A dreamy wondrous look crossed her face when she stopped to gaze at him.

"Come on, Brandy. Let's get out of these clothes and cool off." His glance swept over her and his breath caught when he saw her expression. "Don't look at me like that, honey. I—I can't ease your need anymore than mine today."

Puzzled by his words, she was silent as he ushered her through a wide hall, past several doors to the rear of the vast house. She was shown into an immense bedroom, larger than any she had ever seen. Living in expensive surroundings and never having financial worries had not prepared her for the luxury of Brad's home.

"Like it?"

Awestruck, Brandy raised her eyes, a faint flush staining her cheeks. "It's gorgeous. You just had it redecorated, didn't you?" It was a twin to his suite in Nevada.

"Yes. They finished this week." Brad unsnapped his shirt and rubbed his hand across his chest before pulling the long shirttails from his jeans.

"Why?" Brandy turned to question, her eyes caught by the width of his shoulders and the dark curly hairs across his chest. She looked away when he unbuckled his belt, pulled it from the loops, and dropped it casually on a table.

Brad sat down, reaching to pull each boot off, dropping it with a soft thump on the deep carpeting. His socks followed in short order.

Oh, Lord, she thought. *He's undressing as calmly as if I weren't in the room. Doesn't he realize how it affects me?*

"Why? Because I wanted you to come to me in my home as beautifully as you did in Las Vegas. My mind has been filled with your image walking across that carpeting, your arms outstretched. When I laid your creamy skin against the black satin sheets on the raised bed, I wanted it again. So much so you'll never know."

Brad's voice deepened with the force of his emotions. She never knew she had touched him so. Stirred by his declaration, she walked forward. He had removed his shirt and was standing barefoot, his chest bared, his long legs clad in tight narrow jeans. He had never looked more masculine or appealing to her.

He remained still as her hands clasped his waist, her face buried in the dark hair covering his chest. It tickled her nose as she inhaled the scent of his body. He smelled of sweat—a clean male odor she found a heady experience. Embracing his strong back, she placed kisses across his neck, pleased when she felt him shudder.

"What if you hadn't found me, Brad?"

His hands gripped her waist, holding her away from his chest. Her lips tormented his aroused senses.

"Impossible. I was determined to bring you to my home. Nothing would stop me from finding you." His voice grew harsh, his eyes shimmered with fire in their depths.

She listened as he explained his need in a raspy voice.

"I was torn apart with the sound of your voice, the taste of your sweet mouth, and the feel of your satiny limbs clinging to my hips. Your memory drove me to find you!"

"But—but how did you?"

"With great difficulty! That damn brassy wig you negligently left behind was your downfall."

Brandy leaned against his arms, placing a series of rapid kisses on his iron-hard biceps as he held her away from his body.

"Quit that, Brandy!"

"Like that, huh?" she mimicked his words, before attempting it again. He turned her around and gave her a sharp swat on her buttocks.

"Liking is too mild a word for any caress you give me."

"Go on," she pleaded, rubbing her stinging bottom.

"The fine details are unimportant. Fortunately the wig was expensive and eventually traced back to a Mrs. Harcourt—I damn near had a heart attack hearing you were married—who had charged it to her account. I flew to the New York wholesaler, and from then on it was a slow process of elimination. If it had been a cheap off-the-rack wig, I would have had troubles. The fact that you purchased it the day prior to your trip and the saleslady knew you enabled me to locate you as soon as I did."

Brandy stared at Brad, tears brimming her eyes on learning he cared enough from that first meeting to trace her.

"Get ready for a swim, Brandy. I'm still hot and sweaty."

"I—I like you that way," she told him in a soft voice.

"Damn it, Brandy! Don't you think I don't want to lay you on my own bedspread and make love to you too? I've agonized each night picturing your body beneath mine on top the silky alpaca fur. But get!"

"Where?" she asked, looking around to orient herself with the unfamiliar room.

"Here, in my dressing room, in yours, or in our adjoining bathroom. I don't care, but move it, honey, or I'll strip you myself." Brad reached to his waistband, unsnapping his slacks, indifferent to her presence.

With a quick spurt Brandy fled into the nearest room, shutting the wide paneled door with a bang. "Darn him," she grumbled. "He's not embarrassed over one single thing. He is so casual about his nudity . . . as if it's natural to walk around undressed."

Her fingers fumbled as she stripped the new western clothing from her body. Standing nude before the wall mirrors, she was careful to avoid her reflection, aware she had forgotten to bring in her bathing suit. She glimpsed a short toweling robe draped over a brass rack and slipped into it before returning to the bedroom.

She heard a loud splash and, looking through the opened glass doors, saw Brad swimming in the pool. Long drapes had covered the doors, hiding the beauty of his pool. It was like an oasis, with large rocks placed around three sides to form a natural-looking pond, with waterfalls, exotic plants, and smaller palms. It was perfect, the high adobe wall giving it total privacy.

Entranced by the unexpected beauty, Brandy walked forward, Brad's large robe hanging about her petite body in deep folds. She watched as he swam with vigorous energy from one end to the other. He was as at ease in the water as he was on his horse. Probably good at tennis, racquetball, and hang gliding too, she mused.

Brad noticed her lingering in the opened doors. Holding to the edge at the deep end, he shook water from his eyes before calling out, "Get in here, woman! I want you to exercise the stiffness from your limbs."

"I don't know what you did with my bathing suit," she told him, explaining her reason for the delay.

"Forget the damn thing. I'll probably just take it off you anyway." Laughing at her expression, Brad told her where to find it, then returned to his quick laps of the pool with long strokes.

Brandy dressed quickly in the new bikini made of soft knit jersey in vibrant emerald-green. The bits of cloth hugged her figure, suddenly seeming more daring than when she tried it on in the exclusive Palm Springs boutique.

Chin uptilted, hands clenched, daring Brad to make a personal comment, she walked to the edge of the pool. The brick deck was hot beneath her feet as she hesitated at the deep end.

Brad swam another leisurely lap before motioning for her to get in. A brief glance and he continued without comment. Peeved now because he hadn't said anything, she dove off the side. The shock of the cold water caused a shiver to run through her body as it cooled her heated flesh in one plunge.

Brad stopped, arm braced on the edge, watching as Brandy swam from end to end. Her strokes were smooth, each motion as graceful as he knew it would be. He was pleased that she was uncaring that her hair got wet, enjoying the sensuous look of the thick dark strands swirling across her back.

Brandy swam to Brad and hooked her arm on the edge as she caught her breath. Her eyes sparkled with excitement, her face flawless in the overhead sun, her hair streaming in wet waves around her forehead and ears before clinging to her shoulders.

"This is perfect, Brad. I feel like a pampered princess in this oasis of beauty."

"You look like a happy princess. Your eyes are a deep velvet, the depths inviting me to take you to my tent and ravish your creamy body until you plead for mercy."

"Didn't happen to see a Rudolph Valentino movie, did you?" she chuckled, amused by his leering glance and attempts to scare her.

"Maybe one or two." He laughed, his look changing to one of loving indulgence.

"We've come a long way, Brad. You're apt to find a woman will now drag a man to her own tent until he cries uncle. Women's lib and all that—" Her words were broken off as he placed both broad palms on her face, cupping it tenderly while she clung to the tile. Her heart pounded, her stomach tightened, as the now familiar feeling of languorous sensuality invaded her body.

"Would you cry for mercy? Or would you enjoy it equally? Share my pleasures until we're both exhausted?"

Brad's sudden mood changes puzzled her. He alternated between deep introspective moods of passion, then suddenly thrust her away or changed the subject.

"Answer me, Brandy. Was it just my imagination in Las Vegas that I had found a women with needs as strong as mine? Are you real or a dream?"

"I—I—"

With a groan Brad took her mouth, devouring her lips in a hungry kiss.

She parted her lips and, letting go of the ledge on the inside of the pool, wrapped her arms around his cool, wet shoulders. Unheedingly they sank below the water. Her mind whirled, uncaring that her lungs were starved for air. Slowly they returned to the surface, and without moving completely out of their embrace, they paddled a few feet to the lower water, where Brad was able to touch bottom.

With Brad's limbs entwined with hers, his arms holding her to the firmness of his broad body, her only thoughts were of her need. Her response proved to him that she was equal in her requirements for physical gratification. Her latent sensuality was demanding release—release he had given her with tender regard.

"Your response to my kiss answered my question more than anything else could have," Brad said, his chest heaving. "Yes, my lovely Brandy, you will be my equal." His bronze skin glistened, his hair as black as pitch, his eyes a smoldering charcoal, when he ground out harshly, "I want you now!"

Brandy smiled, thinking she would burst with the delirious feeling of knowing she could cause Brad's towering body to tremble. His desire was the balm she needed for her bruised femininity. She leaned forward, pressing kisses on his wet neck.

His hands slid down her spine, pressing her hips forward. Brandy suddenly realized that he was not wearing a suit: his hardened body was as forceful as his personality.

Brad shuddered at the contact, his hands quivering as his finger stroked her flushed face, stopping on her parted lips. He took her mouth in a short hard kiss. Damn the doctor. He wanted her now, not in some distant future. But he couldn't take her.

"Time for lunch!" he blurted out, breathing deeply in an effort at self-control.

With a quick twist Brad swam across the pool, then climbed the ladder to walk to his room.

Brandy clung to the ledge, watching openmouthed as he left her. One hard kiss, a look of unfulfilled passion, and abrupt departure.

"You're nuts, Mr. Brad Lucas!" she complained, swimming across the pool to climb out. She followed his wet footprints into the house, noticing they led into a room whose door was securely closed.

Upon returning to the luxurious bathroom, Brandy found shampoo, entered the shower, and within minutes was standing wrapped in a soft bathsheet. She didn't want to put her riding clothes back on, but she had left Brad's terry-cloth robe by the pool.

Brad knocked once and entered wearing only a towel around his hips. He eyed her silently, handed her a package, and said, "Your robe's in here. I took the liberty of picking a dress for tonight, some underwear—it was all so sensual—shoes, and a lounging robe."

Brandy took the package, gaping as he looked her over thoroughly before leaving with a sharp admonition to hurry up.

"I'm starving, and you can help me rustle up some lunch."

Brandy toweled her body dry and withdrew clothes to wear. She smiled at his choice: a set of expensive French underwear in black nylon trimmed with Versailles lace.

She felt cool, fastidiously clean, and starved. Her stomach was complaining over the lack of breakfast. She touched her body, thinking of their child growing, the tiny

167

embryo safe and warm. It was already a living culmination of their love.

An instant later she entered the kitchen area. Her make-up was impeccable; her hair drying in soft waves, shining beneath the recessed lighting; and her silk robe clinging in amber print around her limbs. The décolleté neckline and short sleeves were perfect for the coolness of the air-conditioned home.

She looked around but saw no sign of Brad.

CHAPTER NINE

Brad walked into the room, two bottles of wine clasped easily in the fingers of one hand. He looked relaxed, in tan slacks and a dark brown short-sleeve knit shirt. His hair fell in unruly waves across his forehead as if he hadn't bothered to comb it.

"It's about time, Brandy. What would you like for lunch? Lobster, shrimp Louie, prime filet mignon? You name it."

"Hamburger."

"Hamburger? That's a surprise." He set the wine on the wide tiled counter, reaching to take two glasses down from the leaded-glass cupboard overhead. "Fine with me. I'll open my favorite Beaujolais wine, then."

"Excellent." Brandy walked to the huge built-in refrigerator, enchanted that she could fix their first meal. Working in harmony, Brandy placed thick ground-round patties on an indoor grill while Brad set their plates on a wide kitchen counter. Leather stools with padded arms stood on tall wrought-iron legs and lined one side.

The aroma of grilling choice beef soon permeated the room. Brandy's fingers were deft as she sliced tomatoes, sweet red onions, sharp cheddar cheese, and crisp kosher pickles. An accomplished cook, she mixed mayonnaise with a small amount of chili sauce and spread the mixture on toasted sesame seed rolls.

Arranging the charcoal-broiled patties on the bottoms of the rolls, she tasted a bite of melted cheese from one patty, then stacked on crisp lettuce leaves and the toppings. "The aged cheddar's yummy."

She walked to the bar, placed the two plates down, then hoisted her hips gingerly onto the padded stool.

Brad looked at the tempting sandwich before placing the two halves together. With a wink he teased, "Here goes, woman." He bit the juicy hamburger and, chewing with slow deliberation, glanced toward Brandy. "I'll have to put these on my coffee shop menu. I'll call them Brandy Burgers. They'll be a sell out." He took another bite before asking, "What else can you cook?"

"Anything that's not too fancy. Do you like banana nut cake?" *If he does, I'll bake him one every day,* she thought.

"Crazy about it."

"Maybe I'll bake you one sometime, then," she told him casually, taking her first bite of the succulent sandwich.

Sipping red wine, enjoying the tasty burger, and talking, Brandy thought about her godfather. She had spent hours worrying over the best way to tell him about Brad. He would never understand. Plus Daniel and Denise. What, she wondered, did she owe Brad about that part of her life? Everything or nothing?

"Tell me about your marriage, Brandy," Brad prompted, correctly reading her thoughts.

Brandy set her unfinished sandwich on the plate and turned to Brad, her eyes showing her indecision. "I can't, Brad. Not even to you. I'm—I'm sorry." Her lashes lowered and she stepped down to clear up the lunch dishes.

Angered by her constant refusal to tell him the reasons

170

for her platonic marriage and explain her daughter's parentage, he forced himself to keep his voice calm. "I intend to find out, Brandy—preferably before our marriage. But your evasiveness will not delay it one second. Have you thought of a way to explain us to the colonel?"

Brandy's back stiffened as she placed the last dish in the cupboard before making a final swipe over the counter with a damp cloth.

"No." She clenched the edge of the tile, head bowed, back to Brad. "Will you give me more time?"

"No. We marry in seven days. One week from today at this time you will be my wife—with the colonel's approval or not."

Brad walked to his living room to pace back and forth. His windows overlooked the city of Palm Springs, baking in the noon sun. Heat waves shimmered in the distance, but their energy did not equal that caused by his rising anger. Damn Brandy. She had twisted him around her little finger. He was a slave to her amber eyes and innocent look, but he refused to let her procrastinate.

He flexed his broad shoulders, contemplating his life, now in sudden turmoil. Alone with Brandy and he couldn't even make love to her. His need to spend a day in her company was backfiring. She was like a drug invading his bloodstream with increasing potency and he needed constant reassurance that she felt the same.

Curiosity about her marriage was eating his insides. Her stubborn refusal to confide in him hurt like a festering wound.

"Brad."

Her soft voice interrupted his bitter thoughts. She was so beautiful. He needed Brandy, and in seven days she would be his. One long week of turbulence.

171

He had questioned the colonel and James until he felt he knew everything about her life from the day she was born until her marriage. Before the week was up, he would find out what he wanted to know. With or without her narrative!

Upset by the agitation visible on Brad's face, Brandy stood in the foyer, hesitant about what to do next.

"Brad, could we call a truce for the balance of the day? This constant fluctuation of caring is eating at me too."

Brad heard the agony in her voice and went to her. She ran to meet him and clung to his waist. "Forgive me, darling," he whispered into her ear. "I'm taking out my frustrations on you."

He cupped her chin, tilting it upward to enable him to take her mouth. His kiss was hard, love tightly controlled.

He drew away, placing his arm around her waist to guide her down the hall. His home was so large, it took the rest of the afternoon to see every detail. She admired his collections, told him about her watercolors, many of them by well-known artists and extremely valuable. The wide hallway and far wall in his bedroom were ideal for their display.

Brad checked the time, a smile tugging his lips as he spoke. "If our life passes by as fast as today has, we'll be a gray-haired old couple in no time."

She looked at his pitch-black hair, trying to imagine it streaked with silver. "You're going to be a handsome devil when you're older, Brad."

"When I'm older?"

"Yes. By then you will have settled down and won't be so volatile. Easier for me to control."

"I disagree, my love. The day I die my blood will still be stirring for you." His voice was serious, eyes lingering

172

on her gown as if imagining her shape beneath. "Get your fancy clothes on, woman. I'm taking you wining and dining."

"Which do you prefer? My cowgirl clothes or this robe?"

"Neither. Wear the dress I picked out for you while you were getting ready this morning. A deep red in soft clinging material with a neckline that can be pulled down easily so I can kiss your shoulders."

"You are a snoop, Brad. It's a new dress that I purchased downtown. Incidentally, I'm not thrifty. Palm Springs has some excellent stores. Even an I. Magnin's."

"No more wigs, please. I love that dark mane of yours and don't want it hidden beneath anything. Hat, scarf, or wig!"

Brandy spent the next hour getting ready for her evening with Brad. His bathroom had an immense sunken tub, contoured for comfort, with whirlpool jets. She luxuriated in the warm water redolent with bubble bath, until the last lingering stiffness from her horseback riding left.

She twisted back and forth in front of the mirrors, trying to see if she had missed one detail in her grooming. Makeup perfect, lipstick and nail polish matching the color of the dress, hair brushed into smooth feather waves.

Her new dress was soft jersey. A ruffled neckline could be pulled down to bare her shoulders or left up with equal chic. Its blouson top hugged her waist, its soft skirt ruffled on the hem as on the short sleeves. Her only jewelry was the gold chain with Brad's ring nestled between her breasts and a dainty gold watch encircled with diamonds.

Satisfied that she was ready to meet Brad, she walked to the living room. Brad, gazing out the front window, turned as she called to him. He wore a Royal Tussah pure

173

silk sport coat in oatmeal with darker slacks and a white silk shirt opened at the neck with casual elegance. His virile good looks caused her stomach to knot, the inevitable starting of desire.

He walked forward, his eyes surveying her from wavy hair to sandals as they smoldered with primitive savagery.

"You're beautiful, darling. I'm torn between wanting to show you off and hide you forever from all mankind."

"Let's show me off. I'm starving, plus you told me earlier you would take me dancing. I haven't danced in years."

"Good. I don't like the thought of any man ever having held you."

The luxurious Lincoln Continental eased into the parking foyer of the Spanish restaurant within minutes. Leaving it for the valet to park, they entered. Brad was greeted effusively, escorted to a choice table, and given the wine list.

Unhurried, replete with wine, good food and Brad's attentive consideration, Brandy was in a glow of happiness.

Brad had ordered *alcachofas rellenos con sardinas,* an unusual appetizer of sardine-stuffed artichokes. The entrée was a steaming pan of *paella de la Costa Brava.* This colorful dish was a succulent bowl of chicken, sausage links, haddock, prawns, small clams, rice, peas, and spices, whose flavors intermingled to make a savory meal. Brad, aware of Brandy's sweet tooth, ordered *rosquillas,* small doughnutlike fried cakes with a butter and powdered-sugar topping. Eaten hot, they were delicious.

Watching as Brandy ate the last sweet, Brad laughed affectionately.

"For a tiny creature you have a remarkable appetite."

"That, Mr. Lucas, is a definite faux pas. No gentleman would comment on a lady's cravings for food."

"Agreed, but I never said I was a gentleman. Now let's go to a nightclub, watch some entertainment, and work off some of your dinner on the dance floor." Laughing at her outraged expression, he guided her out the entrance with a possessive hand on her waist.

Within minutes they had traveled to an exclusive nightclub, were again shown to a choice table and seated. The darkened room was noisy, filled with cigarette smoke and well dressed people. It reminded her of Las Vegas and the changes in her life since that moment.

Brad's personality was so forceful, he blocked out Daniel's memory for hours at a time, making it more dim each day.

"Don't think about Daniel when you're with me, Brandy."

"How did you know?"

"You get a haunted look in your eyes that I haven't learned to cope with yet. Tonight is our night, and as far as I feel right now, he never existed. In my life or yours."

"But I—"

"Watch the show. I don't even want to hear the man's name now." Brad reached sideways, cupping her chin and placing a swift kiss on her parted lips, his arm remaining around her shoulders as they relaxed in the large booth.

"Brad Lucas, you old son of a gun." Their heads turned at the interrupting voice. "I haven't seen you in a couple of months or more." The good-looking man hovering over their table greeted Brad with obvious affection, his eyes lingering on Brandy in appreciation of her loveliness.

Brad stood up, shaking hands as he introduced Brandy to his friend Logan West and offered to buy him a drink.

Brandy scooted over, allowing Logan room to sit down. He was as big as Brad, with copper-colored hair and deep blue eyes. It was clear that Brad socialized with an affluent circle of friends.

"Are you alone, Logan?" Brad asked curiously. "If you are, it will be the first time," he continued pointedly. "Incidentally I'm warning you off now. Brandy's mine."

"Hmm, that sounds permanent. For a man who acted like a drain cleaner—worked fast and left no ring—you must have found quite a lady." Logan surveyed her intently, eyes mischievous.

"Don't listen to him, Brandy. He thinks that since he's never been caught he's invincible. There will come a time, believe me." Logan laughed as Brad asked him who he was with.

"Here she comes now. Mrs. Mitzi Castleman." They all looked up to see a statuesque red-haired woman approach the table. Her hair was styled elaborately, stiff with spray, but she was lovely, with a full figure and long slim legs.

"Sexy, isn't she?" Logan asked without embarrassment.

"Extremely," Brad answered, his eyes glancing with boredom over the woman's blatant curves.

As Logan made the introductions Mitzi smiled, ignored Brandy, and cooed over Brad as he stood courteously. She placed her hand on Brad's, tracing the taut skin with a fingernail, as she fluttered her eyelashes.

Logan smiled, unconcerned that Mitzi was flirting with his friend.

Brandy seethed. She hated her on sight. False eyelashes too, she thought as Mitzi poured the charm on Brad.

Amused by Brandy's obvious irritation, Brad returned Mitzi's smiles, adding a few remarks of his own.

Logan's eyes twinkled as he watched the interplay

before interrupting his date. "Sit down, Mitzi, you're blocking Brandy's view of the floorshow."

Mitzi eased her shapely hips next to Logan, flashing him a bright smile, her hand lingering on his gold watch.

"Brandy is like you, Mitzi. She's widowed. You two have a lot in common," Brad pointed out drolly.

Brandy placed a well-aimed heel on Brad's toe. Imagine telling that overblown amazon that they had something in common.

Mitzi turned limpid eyes on Brandy, asking in a bored voice, "Oh, was your husband rich and old too?"

"Actually no, Mitzi. I understand he was rich and young," Brad answered, his hand slipping beneath the table to grip Brandy's knee, delighting in her unexpected resentment of Logan's date.

"Ooh . . . that's the best kind." Mitzi giggled, leaning toward Brad, her dress top exposing more than a decent amount of bosom.

That's probably false too. Brandy fumed, surprised by her sudden temper and unusual dislike for another person.

"What do you do for a living, Logan?" Brandy asked, wanting to break up the conversation centered between Brad and Mitzi.

"I'm a real estate broker, Brandy."

"A good one too. He told me to get *a lot* when I was young," Brad teased, laughing out loud when his blatant innuendo dawned on Brandy and her face flushed in surprise.

Logan laughed with Brad as Mitzi looked from one to the other, not understanding their joke.

"Excuse us, please, I promised Brandy a dance and I always like to please the ladies." Brad took her arm, assisting her from the booth. He pulled her into his arms and

177

bent to her ear, biting it as he laughed. "Jealous, you tantalizing bad-tempered witch?" He nibbled on her ear, whispering love words, as they danced in the darkened room, his hand stroking her spine lazily.

Brandy's temper seethed. Pushing against him, she blurted out angrily, "Darn it, Brad. You're a male nympho! Drooling all over that . . . thing!"

"Nympho?" he laughed, enjoying her little body and fiery expression.

"Well, what do they call a male nymphomaniac?"

"Hot." He laughed even louder, noticing her flushed face, never missing a step as they swayed to the slow music.

"That's a terrible word," Brandy said, enjoying the dance despite his outrageous verbal interchange.

"Good a word as any. My blood is always heated near you, my body always hot to take you."

"Shush, Brad. You're awful," she scolded, looking to see if anyone overheard their conversation.

He lowered his head to nip her earlobe, his hands clasped behind her back so she couldn't move out of his hold. "Don't be a stuffy prim little maiden, Brandy. I heard you giggle at my joke about the lot. Even women can enjoy a risqué story without losing any of their feminine qualities if it's not too crude."

"Okay, you win."

They danced in silence, yet she was so aware of his touch, it was painful to bear. Glancing covertly beneath her lowered lashes, she scrutinized his face. His jaw showed determination, his lips sensual tenderness, but his darkened eyes were filled with formidable strength.

They walked in silence back to the table when the song ended. Brandy sat down, purposely avoiding the invitation in Mitzi's eyes as they lingered on Brad. Man-hungry beast! Brandy thought.

"That was good exercise," Brad commented, giving Mitzi a smile before ordering a round of drinks for the four of them.

"Only exercise Mitzi gets is running out of money," Logan teased, his eyes filled with mirth, knowing Mitzi wouldn't catch on.

Brandy smiled at Logan as he asked her to dance, sliding from the booth, her chin tilted as she passed Brad. She was amazed by the change in Logan as they danced. His devilment ended, his voice became deep, the conversation serious. He was interested in Brandy's relationship with Brad, and she found out about his complex sales agency.

"Doesn't it bother you when Mitzi flirts with Brad?" she blurted out after dancing through another song.

"Not in the least, Brandy. Mitzi is not a woman a man could have a meaningful relationship with. She's fairly agreeable, good to look at, and always ready to go to bed."

"Oh, dear. I asked for that, didn't I?"

"Yes. You and she are worlds apart, Brandy. You have a look of wedding rings, babies, and monogamy." Logan was an excellent dancer and determined to keep her on the floor long enough to delve into her meeting with Brad. A meeting she did not relate the slightest detail about.

"Better take you back now. My friend is shooting daggers into my back for keeping his girl away from him. I'm envious of you and Brad. The sparks that fly between the two of you hint at an exciting relationship. One that's good in bed as well as out of it."

"Logan, you are as blunt as Brad. I've never met anybody like either one of you before."

He laughed, his white teeth, sun-bronzed skin, and copper hair a striking combination.

"That comes from being in the Marines together. We were one hell of a team."

They watched another nightclub act, sat around for two hours exchanging social gossip, while Brandy avoided Brad and drank more than she should have.

As Brandy became morose Mitzi sparkled. In her glory seated at a table with two handsome, affluent men, she ignored Brandy completely, which was fine with both of them.

After sitting through a slow-dance number, watching Brad laugh at Mitzi, his hand resting on her naked back while they swayed to the music, she had had enough.

"Excuse me, Logan, but I think I'll call a cab and return to my hotel. I've developed a beastly headache."

"No need to call a taxi. Brad will be finished in a moment or I'll take you home."

"I hate her, Logan. I detest your girl friend," Brandy blurted out, filled with jealousy. "Look at her lean on Brad."

"Oh, honey, you are priceless. I've never met a woman honest enough to admit how she feels about another female. Don't worry about Brad. We both know how to pick the gold from the dross. Brad just happened to be the first to find the gold."

Brandy looked at Logan's face, a smile lighting her face with etheral beauty. "Mr. West, if I didn't love that horrible monster Mr. Lucas, I'd give Mitzi a run for you."

"That's a girl, Brandy. Watch old Brad come running now."

Logan stood up, taking Brandy's elbow to assist her from the table. He placed a possessive hand on her waist before turning to his friend and date. "If you'll excuse us, I'm going to run Brandy to her hotel. She has a headache."

Brad's eyes darkened, looking from one to the other, uncertain if they were serious or not. "The hell you are, Logan. And keep your hands off her unless you're dancing."

Brad nodded a curt good-bye to Mitzi, took Brandy by the waist, glared at Logan, and left the nightclub with long determined strides.

"Stop, you big bully, I've got a stitch in my side," Brandy scolded, though pleased to be away from Mitzi. She knew Logan would be her friend for life. He was honest, direct, and would do anything for Brad.

"You deserve it. Taking off with my friend and leaving me with that man-eating redhead." Brad shoved her gently into the front seat of the car before getting behind the wheel.

She could feel his anger and was pleased by his sudden display of ownership. It helped soothe her previous temper.

"Where are we going now?"

"For a drive. I need to cool off a little before I drop you off at the hotel. A long drive is my therapy for frustration."

Brandy was content to remain silent. She had drunk too much, for the first time in her life, and did not like the light-headed feeling. With a sigh she eased against the cushioned seat, her head nodding until she thought about Brad's earlier joke.

"Well, did you?" she blurted out furiously.

"Did I what? What the hell are you blabbing about?"

"Get—get a lot."

"My God, that conversation was three hours ago. To answer you in one word: yes, naturally I did."

Jealousy filled Brandy's mind as she imagined Brad with other women, his body taking theirs as it had hers. "That's four words."

"My beautiful wife-to-be, the 'lot' I got—was nothing but a training program for the real thing. A necessary release. You have nothing to fear. My fidelity will be unquestionable."

"Even with redheaded amazons?" she whispered, appeased by his vehement proclamation.

"Especially with redheads. Now shut up while I drive."

Brandy relaxed, enjoying the drive after hearing Brad's assurances of his devotion. She leaned her head back, content to be with him as he drove in a wide loop toward Indio and back. She moved to Brad's side and, closing her eyes, rested her head against his broad shoulder comfortably.

Brad circled in front of his hotel and parked in the private space reserved for him. It was two o'clock in the morning, his guests having retired for the night.

Brandy fluttered her lashes, aware that the car had stopped. She sat up, glancing at Brad in the light of a streetlight. His expression was grim as he watched her.

Catching her off guard he grated out, "Tell me about Daniel now, Brandy. Why? Why didn't he take you? Was he impotent?"

Brandy closed her eyes, thinking of Daniel, her voice barely audible. "No, Brad. He was very sexually active in fact."

"He was?" Brad was stunned, and he prompted her to continue.

"I will not say another thing, Brad. If the evening is

going to end with an inquisition, then I prefer to go to my room now."

"No inquisition, then. We'll end it like this!" Brad's hands gripped her shoulders, their touch a warning that he had the power to make her bow to his demands, that he would be undeterred in his quest to probe into the intimate details of her marriage.

Without warning he took her lips, his kiss demanding. A mature man's caress: his tongue parted her lips easily to penetrate her moist inner mouth. The intimacy evoked wave after wave of sensation so potent, her body trembled. His touch, the stroking fingers moving across her full breasts, was causing unbearable ecstasy to flow through her veins.

He pulled her dress off her shoulder, low enough to expose one swelling breast. He fondled it tenderly before bending her along the seat until his mouth could replace his hand, sucking her naked curve to pulsating awareness, the nipple a hard bud beneath his tongue.

Brandy gasped, her fingers gripping his dark hair in convulsive tremors as he plundered the sensitive point of her breast before returning to her mouth.

Brandy was breathless with the sudden assault on her emotions. Brad was ruthless in his determination to mold her to his will. His hands traced the contours of her body before sliding to her face to cup it in the warmth of his broad palms.

Brandy's resistance melted, all thought of rebellion leaving as one insidious thumb rubbed back and forth across her mouth. Her lips softened unconsciously when Brad's tongue invaded her parted lips with slow deliberate motions. The probing continued until she returned it with equal fervor.

Pulling away from her quivering body, Brad stared. Her skin looked pearllike, luminous in the tall overhead lamp.

Slowly his hands lifted to cradle her white face.

"You have six days, Brandy. Only six days to tell the colonel."

CHAPTER TEN

Sobs tore at Brandy's throat early that same morning as she looked through her purse for the phone number to the gynecologist Brad had contacted. She had refused to allow him to make an appointment but she needed one desperately now.

She found it and quickly dialed the phone with trembling fingers. Impatiently she waited for the receptionist to answer.

"Dr. Fortner please," she asked nervously, her lower lip trembling.

"The doctor is with a patient now. May I tell her who's calling, please?" the calm secretary answered.

Her? Brandy thought. *Brad actually talked with a female doctor about me.*

"Mrs. Harcourt. I had an appointment two weeks earlier and—er—couldn't keep it. Now I need one."

The young secretary confirmed a sudden cancellation. If Brandy could be at their office in thirty minutes, the doctor would be glad to talk with her.

Within five minutes Brandy was waiting in the lobby for her taxi. She had avoided her godfather's room, not wanting to see him until after her examination. She didn't want to see anyone, especially Brad, until her suspicions were confirmed.

One hour later Brandy had completed dressing. Leaving the doctor's examining room, she was shown to the consulting office, her face still pale with shock.

"Sit down, Mrs. Harcourt. I would like to talk with you a minute. Obviously you are shaken by the news that you are not pregnant."

Brandy looked at the doctor's pretty face. In her late forties, with fashionably gray-streaked hair, she was a charming woman, with a soft voice and keen eyes.

"I feel rather foolish, Doctor. I was certain I was pregnant. I have always had regular menses and when I missed for over five weeks . . . well . . ." Brandy's voice drifted off.

"Our bodies work in strange ways, Brandy. You have been under unusual strain these last few months. The double funeral, abrupt move from your home, worry about your godfather, could all cause temporary delay. You are a healthy young woman, but the chance of becoming pregnant in one encounter with Mr. Lucas was remote."

"He told you about that?" Brandy questioned, stunned that Brad had been so forthright with a woman.

"My dear, Mr. Lucas told me the entire story. He went into detail about seducing you despite your objections." Dr. Fortner's voice was professional as she continued confidentially. "He loves you very much."

Brandy smiled, her eyes wide, voice faltering briefly. "These past two weeks have been rather platonic for a man in love."

The doctor laughed before explaining. "Didn't he tell you about our talk?"

"No."

"Mrs. Harcourt, your fiancé came storming into my office two weeks ago to make an appointment for your prenatal exam. Incidentally, I could have saved you both stress if you had let me examine you earlier. But to continue, Mr. Lucas asked me bluntly if an active sexual relationship now would endanger the safety of your child."

A soft flush tinged Brandy's cheeks. Brad continued to amaze her. He wanted her, was determined to make love to her during the three weeks before their marriage, yet cared enough about their supposed child to get medical approval.

"Don't be embarrassed, my dear. You are fortunate to have a man eager to bring you physical happiness. Many of my patients would be fine if they had satisfying sexual relations. He is unique in that his needs are secondary to your pleasure."

Brandy's voice faltered momentarily. "What did you tell him?"

"I told him to leave you alone until I had examined you."

"But why? Don't most people continue their intimate association?" Brandy questioned with a puzzled look.

"Certainly. But Mr. Lucas is not most people. He confessed it would be impossible to make gentle love to you, that you were too volatile in bed together, and he doubted if he would let you out of his room for the three weeks prior to your intended marriage."

"I can't believe him," Brandy blurted out, her lashes downcast, bright spots of color on her cheeks.

"Don't be embarrassed, Brandy. You are to be envied. Mr. Lucas is a handsome man and most important an honest open one. He told me it would be easier to stay

187

away than tamp his needs." The doctor's smile was friendly, eyes revealing a sense of humor. "You are a lucky young woman."

Brandy laughed softly, her eyes taking on the slumberous look of remembered passions.

"I know, Dr. Fortner. That explains his wavering moods these last few days." Especially yesterday, Brandy thought, remembering her offer and his emphatic refusal.

"I have another appointment now," Dr. Fortner said, standing to walk with Brandy from her consulting room. "It has been nice meeting you, Brandy. I imagine you will be a regular patient after your marriage."

Thanking her, Brandy walked to the front desk, paid the bill and walked the short distance to town. It was another warm day and the thought of a frosty drink before returning to the hotel was an irresistible temptation.

Brandy chose a cozy family restaurant and walked to the back to a small booth for two. She sipped a refreshing glass of iced tea while waiting for a chef's salad, undecided what to do.

She needed time to regain a modicum of composure, an art she had learned well during the preceding months. Life was complex again. Her godfather would have to be told and would be saddened by the news.

Knowing she wasn't pregnant would change everything between her and Brad. There was no need for them to even marry. Yet his deadline for marriage was not set for the birth of his expected child but his need to see their relationship brought into the open with the colonel and James.

Brandy picked through the slivers of meat and cheese, listlessly eating her salad. The food was good, the place filled with local diners, but she was unable to finish. Pushing the wooden dish aside, she called to the waitress, then paid her bill and walked outside in search of a taxi.

Back in her room, she took a cool shower and changed into comfortable lightweight slacks and a sleeveless blouse, feeling clean and refreshed. Enjoying the air-conditioned comfort away from the blazing sun, she relaxed with a new paperback until it was time to dress for dinner.

Four or five hours would make no difference to Brad or her godfather and would give her much-needed privacy. She had left a message that she was going shopping, and no one would question her absence for the entire day.

Prior to dinner Brandy's godfather phoned to ask if she minded eating dinner alone. He and James had been invited to attend a senior citizens' shuffleboard tournament, followed by an outdoor barbecue.

Brandy was delighted. Since coming to Palm Springs, the colonel was like a new man. The daily mineral sunbaths tanned him and James to a deep brown. They looked fit, and Brandy had even noticed them conversing with some of the more persistent widows. This was the first time she could remember her godfather socializing. He was a private person and was happiest to himself.

Forgetting to inquire about Brad, she phoned her godfather.

"Godfather," she asked without preamble, "have you been in touch with Brad today?"

"Yes, Brandy. He phoned me this morning, just prior to his departure." Her godfather's voice was gruff, attesting to his impatience to be on his way to the tournament.

"Departure for where?" she prompted, an intuitive feeling of unease.

"Not certain, girl, and didn't care to ask. He said something about important business taking him away for several days."

"Did—did he say when he would return?" she asked, her voice hesitant as her mind whirled with the possibilities of what he was doing.

"Told me he would be back in the morning of the sixth day. Why do you care anyway? You haven't spoken two words to the man the last couple weeks. Last time we were together you stormed off from the dinner table in a typical female huff."

"I had a headache," Brandy lied. Her headache was caused by Brad's lack of attention.

"You never used to get headaches. Why are you asking me all these questions anyway? You were with him all day yesterday."

"He didn't say anything about a trip," she whispered back.

"Well, he's gone and so will James and I be if you'll hang up. Don't want to miss nothing, girl. Might even take it up myself soon. Used to be pretty good couple years ago," he bragged.

"Two years! You haven't played shuffleboard for at least ten that I know of." Brandy laughed. Her godfather's concept of time was directly related to his age: always shortened for him and lengthened for his few friends.

"Quit laughing, girl. Only taking up the sport so James can get some exercise. He doesn't do enough."

"I don't agree, Godfather. Taking care of you would be a full-time job for any one person no matter what their age," Brandy teased indulgently, her heart filled with love.

"You are getting too sassy. The only one who has really controlled your impudence is Brad." The colonel's voice softened as he told her, "Missed that boy today, dammit. Ex-Marine, you know?"

"Good-bye, Godfather," Brandy told him respectfully, thinking, *Missed that boy today myself, dammit!*

The next four days followed along the same pattern. Brandy sunbathed by the pool each morning and afternoon, her creamy skin turning a pale gold, which enhanced her youthful beauty. The excellent cuisine, luxurious accommodations, and relaxed atmosphere caused an added bloom in her appearance. A long shopping spree lowered her bank balance further.

Each day she went in the hotel van to their stables. The kitchen staff obliged with fresh carrots, while her hotel room fruit basket needed a daily replacement of crisp apples. Recipient of the treats were Whoa Boy and Gray Witch. They recognized her now, greedily nickering for the apples and especially the carrots, a new treat they relished with each chomp of their powerful jaws.

She wanted to ride, but hesitated without Brad's permission. She had no problem making friends with the stablehands, who were glad to let her groom both animals daily.

Brandy spent an hour each morning with Brad's two horses. They stood patiently, ears flicking, hooves deep in the pungent-smelling pine shavings, while she groomed their silky coats with a soft brush. When their bodies were free of dust, she would comb out their manes and tails into long tangle-free strands, Whoa Boy's a deep chestnut and Gray Witch's a shiny silver-gray. A soft kiss on each velvety muzzle and she was finished.

Her godfather's health improved. He and Brandy shared long conversations each afternoon before his nap

191

and during their evening meal. The rest of the day he was involved with a widening circle of friends.

He would talk for hours with anyone willing to listen to his numerous exploits during World War II. Brandy noticed with amusement that it appeared there was a disproportionate number of single women willing to hear him out. Most of the men had their own tales to relate.

Despite the pleasure of her idle existence she knew she was procrastinating. Brandy paced the living area of her room. She wiped her damp palms down the sides of her dress, her overactive imagination filling her with the possible consequences of her tale.

Would her godfather collapse? She could never forgive herself if her love for Brad caused a serious setback to his fragile health. He had never faltered in his love and attention. She had been treated gently her entire life by a grim, outspoken man whose eyes and voice softened whenever he talked with her. She loved him, each irascible, grumbling bit of his personality.

By noon the following day Brandy knew she could not delay any longer. She had put it off too long. Brad was scheduled to return sometime in the morning. He had told her three weeks earlier they would marry on tomorrow's date, that arrangements had been made. If Brandy had not told the colonel by then, he would. His threat was meant to be taken seriously.

Brandy took a deep breath, left her room, and walked down the stairs to her godfather's room. James had gone to town to service the Cadillac and was not expected back for the rest of the afternoon. It was the opportunity Brandy had waited for, dreaded with intense nervousness.

After giving her godfather a kiss on his tanned cheek, she paced back and forth in his room. He was sitting up in bed, wearing a new pair of blue pajamas, his hair tousled and eyes lingering on his goddaughter.

"Tell me what's bothering you, child. I've seen your haunted look these last three weeks. And noticed the way you watch Brad but avoid being alone with him, with the exception of yesterday's outing."

Brandy, her legs threatening to collapse on hearing her godfather's astute observations, sat on the edge of his wide bed. Head bowed, tears streaming down her cheeks, she sobbed in silence, unable to speak a single word.

"You love that boy, don't you, child?"

Brandy raised her face, her eyes a dark velvet amber shade, her dark lashes spiky with tears as she nodded yes.

His gnarled hand reached out, holding her trembling fingers still.

"Listen to me, Brandy. I've never mentioned this to another soul. I loved Daniel's mother for years. She was married to my best friend, and of course I refused to even consider interfering in their marriage."

Brandy held his hand to her cheek briefly before holding it on her lap as she listened raptly.

"When he was killed in the war, I consoled her. It was the first time I had ever held her in my arms. It was torture to me. I ached with passion yet was torn apart with guilt over my feelings.

She was attracted to me soon afterward. Honest about her long marriage, she admitted it had been unsettled from the first. When I confessed I had loved her for years, we both cried bitter tears.

"She wanted to get married immediately; her love was strong enough to face any embarrassment or unkind comment from our friends. I refused her. My guilt and sense of propriety kept us apart for six months."

193

Tears filled his eyes, his voice wavering as he thought of the young girl he had loved so desperately.

"Within a year of our marriage she was dead. Those six months could have been filled with our love, instead they were months of frustration for both of us when they could have been memories to cherish after her death."

Brandy threw herself forward, her head resting on her godfather's lap as she sobbed, her heart overflowing with love.

"Oh, Godfather . . . I love you. I too have been torn apart with guilt. My love for Brad is as different from what I felt for Daniel as night from day."

Tears spilled unchecked down her cheeks as she rose, cradling his hand with deep devotion. His story had torn at her heart. She sympathized with his young wife, knowing how damaging a troubled marriage could be.

Brad's need to face the world openly and to share his passions with long nights of love had caused him constant pain. Brandy was eager to make up to him for the weeks of turmoil—turmoil she had provoked unintentionally.

Brandy kissed her godfather's hand before laying it back on the bed.

"You won't care, Godfather?" she asked, her quiet voice belying the depth of feeling behind the question.

"No, Brandy. I will be proud. In war a man gains a philosophical attitude toward death. Life is for the living, child. Brad is an impatient man. If he loves you, he won't be willing to wait."

"I know, Godfather. He told me the second night we were here that today was the deadline to tell you about our love. If I didn't, he was going to tell you himself."

"Good for the boy. A good Marine won't be intimidated by anything even though I outrank him!"

"He—he told James the day after we checked in that he was going to marry me."

"Why, that old coot James. He never even hinted a thing."

Brandy laughed at her godfather's expression, his eyes as bright as his pajama top. A frown crossed Brandy's face, her thoughts on the next confession she had to make.

"What else is the matter, Brandy? Confide everything to me, child."

"I'm not pregnant," she blurted out, unable to think of an easy way to give him the news.

He looked at his goddaughter, watching pain shadow her eyes. "Did you miscarry?"

"No. I was never pregnant."

"It is for the best, Brandy. Brad is a proud man and would love your child as well as you, but it's best to start fresh. Daniel is your past. Without my son's child you can start marriage as it should be. No entanglements."

"Are you certain you don't care?"

"No, child, I don't mind. I have a feeling it won't be too many weeks before Brad has you pregnant. Probably even give me a black-haired gray-eyed grandson too!"

Brandy wept inside for the secret she must never reveal. Her godfather would never learn of her deception nor would she ever utter a single word from her lips that her marriage with Daniel had not been as happy as he believed.

"I will miss you, Godfather, when you and James return home. Being with the men I love most in the world has made my happiness replete."

"Actually, child, you might not get rid of me. I've enjoyed my time here and never felt better. James and I have made several friendships with people I would miss. I have no business owning a thirteen-room house."

"Would you sell?"

"I might, but I want Brad's advice first. I could buy a mobile home even. Brad will tell me what's best. Right?"

"Right, Godfather. It's a good thing Brad has great big broad shoulders because it appears he has three dependents to care for. You and me and James."

Her godfather chuckled, agreeing that Brad could manage all of them easily.

"He's an ex-Marine, you know," Brandy added mischievously.

"Get out of here, child, and let me take my nap. I think that last remark was meant as an impudent sass."

Brandy placed a brief kiss on his lined face before walking to his bedroom door. She turned, a smile lingering on her face, the haunted look gone from her eyes. Her weeks of worry had been in vain.

Later that night she twisted restlessly in the wide bed. Her evening's cheerfulness had abated when she began to wonder about Brad's reaction when he learned she wasn't pregnant.

Would his feelings change? Teardrops slipped beneath her closed lids as she drifted into a restless sleep.

CHAPTER ELEVEN

Shortly after midnight Brad entered Brandy's room. He flexed his bare shoulders, attempting to ease their stiffness, one hand raised to rub the tension from his forehead.

He was bone weary. The last six days had been spent traveling: in his private jet, an intercontinental 747, or a rented car. Jet lag and lack of sleep were taking their toll.

What he had learned stunned him. He was anxious to talk with Brandy, but it could wait until after their marriage. His needs now were rest and reassurance she was his. This he could get by holding her, knowing she was alongside him the balance of the night.

In twelve hours they would be married. His patience had been stretched to the limits in an attempt to understand the many puzzling aspects of her platonic relationship. Her refusal to relate any details had earned his admiration and his anger. Now he was too weary to think about it.

Familiar with the room, he walked straight to the bed, drenched in moonlight pouring in through the window. He bent to pull back the covers and eased quietly onto the comfort of the thick mattress, his lower body clad in black silk pajama bottoms.

Damn the things, he thought. He had purchased them

in Los Angeles, but because he usually slept nude, they were noticeably uncomfortable. The temptation to take her would be unbearable if he was naked. Tonight sleep was his most important need.

He heard a muffled sob, felt dampness on her cheek as he touched her face. His arms reached beneath her slender body, drawing her to the length of his outstretched form.

"Come closer, darling," he whispered, her scent invading his nostrils with its heady perfume. He could feel his heartbeat increase, the familiar ache in his loins.

Lord, how he loved her! She was unbelievable. Fastidiously clean, exquisitely feminine, had the appetite of a small trucker, and a keen sense of humor that bubbled forth, making her eyes shine like precious jewels.

His dreams had been haunted by her naked body stretched on top of his luxurious alpaca fur spread. She lay there, her arms extended to hold him, her bewitching amber glance filled with expectations of passion to come, beckoning until he would wake.

He never fantasized such passion could be contained in one small female. Brandy made love like each time would be her last. And she was a novice! What the hell would she be like when he showed her the many ways to express her sexuality? The thought was enough to make his heart stop.

His mouth pressed her sleep-softened lips in a gentle kiss. He did not want to rouse her to full consciousness.

Brandy felt Brad's lips touch her mouth. Murmuring incoherently between sobs, she snuggled against his hair-roughened chest, fingers clinging to his back.

Smoothing her hair, he whispered words of love, not understanding her distress. Silky strands tickled his lips as he spoke softly, his face resting on her forehead.

"Don't cry, darling. Please stop."

His hand cupped her head, holding her close, aware the silk pajama pants were no barrier to his desire. Her slinky nightgown had slid up, leaving the entire length of her satiny limbs bare. Her body was warm, soft, and—God help him—receptive.

Brandy burrowed into his neck, parted lips placing frantic kisses in the hollow of his throat and hard collarbone. Tears continued to trickle from her eyes unabated.

He cupped her chin, raising it so he could lick each salty drop from her cheeks.

"Tell me why you are crying, little one. Is it because of our marriage?"

"No . . . no. I told Godfather and he gives us his blessing, but now"—her sobs increased and her body quivered—"you won't want to marry me."

"Why?" Brad's hand stroked up and down her spine, his fingers splayed to fondle with comforting warmth, as he waited for her answer.

"Because I have nothing to give you."

"Nothing? What about our raven-haired gray-eyed child?"

Her tears stopped and her eyes closed as she willed him to go away . . . yet she needed him more than she had ever needed anyone in her life. Her words faltered as she murmured poignantly, "I'm not pregnant. Oh, Brad, it's so awful. I was never carrying your child. Just overwrought."

Brad's astonished voice was filled with concern. "Don't worry, darling. That's no problem. I'll give you black-haired gray-eyed baby sons by the dozen. And when you have enough of them, I will start making chestnut-haired amber-eyed delectable little girls, just like their mother."

Slowly his hands rose to cradle her face before he took her mouth in a long kiss meant to console not arouse.

"My poor little love. You have had one hell of a life for one so young." Hearing her soft sigh, knowing she was comforted by his reassurances, he crooned affectionately.

"Sleep now, darling . . . sleep. We have the rest of our lives to talk."

Cradled in the strength of his hold, Brandy closed her eyes, silken strands of hair spread across his naked shoulders. Brad's chest rose and fell rhythmically as he relaxed, his weary body finally getting long-denied sleep.

Brandy awoke briefly before dawn. Brad's chest was warm against her back: his legs touched the length of her bare limbs; one long arm cradled her close, fingers spread across her abdomen. She let the haze of contentment pull her back into oblivion, soothed by Brad's even breathing.

When she awoke the second time, she was alone in the sunlit room. The faint scent of Brad's after-shave and the indented pillow beside her were convincing evidence that she hadn't been dreaming. Brad had come to her and soothed her fears while holding her through the night. His determination to make her his wife had never faltered.

She sat up quickly, a smile curving her lips, when Brad entered through the communicating door. Balancing a tray on one palm, he walked to the bed and placed it across her lap with an exaggerated flourish, his darkened eyes bright with mischief.

A single red rose, unopened, with glistening drops of dew clinging to its outer petals, lay across a linen napkin. She lifted a silver lid covering a plate of hot creamy scrambled eggs, ham slices, and buttered English muffin halves. A separate silver coffee pot and delicate china cup were the most enticing until she awoke fully.

"Hmm, this looks delicious." Pouring her coffee, she inhaled the rich aroma, then held it out to Brad. "Will you share with me?"

"I'll share everything with you, Brandy. My love, my wealth, my home, and my heart. No coffee though, as I just finished having breakfast with the colonel and James. Eat your breakfast, darling, you'll need your strength for our honeymoon."

"Today?" she questioned breathlessly.

Brad smiled, holding his wrist up to check the time. "It starts in six hours. Put on your best dress, woman. We have an appointment with the minister in exactly three hours."

"Three hours?"

"Yes. We leave Palm Springs as soon as you're ready," Brad explained, watching indulgently as she added a second spoonful of thick strawberry preserves on the muffin.

"Where?" she asked, licking jam off her lips. The action caused Brad to inhale with heightened desire.

"Las Vegas. It seemed fitting, since that's where I fell in love and received your innocence." His voice deepened, the tone husky, as memories of their first encounter entered his mind.

Brandy looked up when his voice changed, explaining, "No. I meant where have you been this past week?"

"I'll tell you later." He watched her closely, admiring her composure. She never acted coy, hadn't worried about sleeping with him, worried about her tousled hair or sleepy face free of makeup.

Brad leaned over the bed to pick up the tray and noticed that one narrow black strap had fallen off her shoulder. With slow deliberation he placed his mouth on the satiny skin, kissing along the curve to her neck. Brandy's indrawn breath stopped him. Damn, he hurt. His thoughts ran ahead: before the day was over he would taste each inch of her body. There were endless erotic pleasures to experience, and by God, he was ready.

"Get dressed, witch. I'm determined to make an honest woman of you, so don't dillydally or I might change my mind."

His laughter echoed through the room as he ducked through the door, the breakfast tray balanced precariously. Brandy playfully threw her fluffy bed pillow at his retreating back but missed.

Later Brandy walked into her godfather's suite, wearing an exquisite ivory lace dress lined with amber silk. The short bias-cut skirt swirled to her knees; the fitted bodice buttoned at the throat and cuffs. The simple style acted as a frame for her petite figure, vibrant chestnut hair, and unique-colored eyes.

She looked at the three men who waited impatiently, her glance lingering on each in turn.

Brad stood to one side, his smoky eyes narrowing, locking with hers, their message bringing a flush to Brandy's cheeks. He was counting the hours until they were alone. His passions were tightly checked now, but the currents between them were electrifying.

He wore a pale gray suit, impeccably tailored to his brawny size, the silk shirt and tie in coordinating colors. He was so handsome, her knees threatened to buckle. His expression of sensual indulgence and blatant need forced her to glance away.

Brandy walked to James and kissed his cheek, then to her godfather, whom she hugged around his narrow waist. Both men wore dark formal suits, their faces a healthy tan from daily mineral baths. The aroma of excessive after-shave brought a smile to her lips. She loved them both.

She placed a kiss on her godfather's lined face, noticing his gray hair stood in spiky tousles, despite the application of extra hair dressing.

"Quit kissing me, child. You'll mess your lipstick. Right, Brad?" His voice was gruff, but Brandy noticed he turned his head, surreptitiously wiping tears from his eyes.

"Right, Colonel," Brad returned quickly. "Come on, gentlemen. My pilot is waiting. His patience is not endless and mine is less."

"That's the Marine in you, Brad," the colonel told him. "Always the first ones there, weren't we, boy?"

The ease with which Brad ushered them out of his hotel, into the waiting car, and to the airport left Brandy breathless. A gleaming private jet waited, its interior as luxurious as Brad's home. Leaving them, Brad went forward to the cockpit, where he sat with the pilot during the swift flight to Las Vegas, giving Brandy time to have a last-moment conversation with her godfather and James.

Within the hour they were married, Brandy held possessively to Brad's side, his gold band circling her finger in back of a flawless diamond solitaire whose brilliance and size left her speechless.

Brad had reserved a suite in Las Vegas, surprising the colonel and James with a minivacation. Their eyes were filled with excitement at the thought of spending three days gambling. Brad's pilot would return to fly them back to Palm Springs.

Tenderness filled her heart at his consideration. His affection for the two men was genuine, patience with them more tolerant than with her.

Hugging her godfather, she blurted out huskily, "I love

you." Tears spilled from her eyes as she kissed him softly on his cheek.

His back was erect, eyes a bright piercing blue as he watched his goddaughter. Happiness filled his heart. She had been a devoted, loving wife to his son, given him a grandchild, and survived their tragic deaths to bring his life new purpose: a boy he loved as if he were his natural father.

"Quit crying, girl. No need for tears today. You're marrying a military man, you know."

"Yes, Godfather, I know." Brandy smiled, hugging his waist. "Is it really true that you and James will be moving into Brad's guest house?"

"Yes. Brad says we military men have to take care of each other. Also"—he shot a look to see if James could hear him—"James needs the mineral baths. He's getting old."

"Godfather!" Brandy admonished him, her eyes enjoying his mischievousness.

"Hush, child. Brad says he'll need James and me to baby-sit in nine months." Her godfather's laugh was loud as he looked from James to Brad to see if they were listening.

Brandy's lashes lowered, a bright flush tinging her face, as she thought of living with a man as volatile and masculine as Brad.

Brandy was guided from the chapel to the waiting taxi, driven to the airport, and returned to Palm Springs a married woman before the afternoon sun had cooled.

She glanced covertly at Brad's face during the drive to his home. He was quiet during their flight. She sensed intuitively that he was troubled. Placing her hand on his thigh, she squeezed it gently. He would tell her in his own time.

Excited laughter filled the living room as Brad carried Brandy across the threshold. Her eyes shimmered, breath catching in her throat as his mouth descended to possess her lips in a hungry kiss. He broke it off abruptly, standing her on her feet.

"Now what?" she teased, watching him tug the knot of his tie loose before pulling it from his neck in one jerk. His hand returned to unbutton his shirt, but his eyes lingered on her figure.

"What a foolish question from a newly married woman to her frustrated husband."

She gave him a crooked smile, chin upraised impudently.

"Get moving, woman—and make certain it's toward our bedroom," he commanded, eyes glinting with mischief.

"In the middle of the afternoon?" she sassed playfully, reveling in his spontaneous humor.

"Middle of the afternoon, early morning, late at night. Before the colonel and James return, you will be able to tell which hour in twenty-four you prefer my lovemaking, because we will damn well try them all!"

"Sexy beast, aren't you?" she squealed as he lunged forward then swept her into his arms and carried her to his room with long forceful strides.

Dumped on top his bed, she giggled, trying to keep her dress from sliding up her thighs.

Brad loomed over her, hands on hips, broad chest heaving. "Well, woman? Do we cool off in the pool before we heat up in bed?"

Scooting into a sitting position, she glared at him. "Darn you, Brad. You're outrageous."

"No, only frustrated and eager to get out of this suit and into—"

"Brad!" she interrupted, afraid what he would say next.

"—the pool. Fooled you, didn't I? Last one in cooks the dinner." Brad shrugged out of his jacket, finished unbuttoning his shirt, and was reaching for his slacks when Brandy rushed to her private dressing room. Her clothes had been placed in the closet and dresser while they were gone. She noticed without surprise that the housekeeper was nowhere in sight.

Adjusting the brief top of her white crochet bikini, she preened before the mirror. Her skin was golden tan from long days basking in the sun, waiting for Brad to return. *At least I look like a local resident now,* she thought, remembering their year-round tans.

She entered their bedroom in time to see Brad walk to the edge of the pool and dive into the deep end with barely a splash. He surfaced, shaking water from his eyes and hair, motioning for her to join him, not a stitch on his body.

Brandy stood on the deck, looking at his wide bronzed shoulders while he tread water, his eyes lingering on each exposed curve.

"Brad, you can't keep running around nude in front of me."

"Why not? You've seen me nude. I've seen all of you, so what's the big deal. Now hush, remove your sexy little white suit and get in the water."

Brandy glared at him, refusing to remove her bikini. Brad's lack of embarrassment about his nudity was comforting, but she still wasn't ready to parade around unclothed, despite their intimacies.

She dove off the edge and swam toward him. Laughing, she reached out to push his head under water, before retreating to the other side in a flurry of whirling water.

In pursuit after letting her duck him, he swam forward. Clasping her shoulders, he pulled her to his chest. She was helpless against his strength as he casually untied her bra and slipped the stretchy panties from her hips.

The tiny pieces of cloth fell to the bottom as Brandy writhed ineffectually to get away from his blatant sexuality. Brad's needs appeared insatiable, which he admitted readily and without shame.

"By God, wife, I thought we'd play around in the cooling water before long relaxing sex in bed."

Brandy clung to his neck, biting his shoulder with gentle nips. Her passions were heightened by contact with his nakedness. His constant touch made her feel wanton, her craving to experience each erotic pleasure increasing as her body relaxed. She felt his mouth kiss the side of her neck, move to her sensitive ear. One broad palm cupped a swelling breast, the other sliding down her spine to pull her round buttock forward, his male need pressed intimately close. Murmuring poignantly, she clasped his face, trembling fingers holding his jaw still while she claimed his lips.

She clung to his neck, gasping for breath, as he carried her from the pool. Their wet bodies dripped, unnoticed, on the bedroom carpet.

"It's your fault, my sensuous wife. Instead of getting a leisurely loving first, it will be wild and exciting like this."

Uncaring that Brandy's hair and body were streaming wet, Brad placed her on the soft fur spread, falling with her. A ragged groan escaped from deep in his throat, his mouth seeking hers eagerly, his sensual hunger out of control.

The primitive savagery of his open mouth and arousing tautness of his lithe body brought a surging response from deep within Brandy's abdomen. His skin seared hers with white-hot fire.

Rippling muscles trembled beneath her fingertips, Brad's back rock hard. Inflamed by her taunting antics in the pool, he swept his hands over the length of her body, lingering on each erogenous zone. She met his hunger with equal intensity, her body's inherent sensuality flowering to full womanhood.

Brad's kiss provided fuel for the flames that had only been tamped—never out—since their first volatile coupling. They satisfied a lack in the other, melting together with fiery satisfaction.

Brandy's body was cradled by the luxurious fur as Brad hovered above her, his hips pinning her quivering limbs beneath him. He cupped her cheeks, staring at the exquisite flush on her passionate face.

She looked at his strong features, entranced by his well-defined mouth. Her lips parted to let her tongue trace the shape of his lips. Finishing the circle, she put the tip of her tongue in his mouth, flicking his teeth until he groaned, crushing her with hot urgency.

"Wife . . . my beautiful wife," he moaned in a ragged voice. "What you do to me should be illegal."

His mouth left hers to nibble a path to her pulsating breasts, inch by inch until he was over the erect peak of her swollen curve.

His male contours surged against her hips as she squirmed to get closer. "You have gorgeous breasts, so very beautiful—" His words were broken off as he took the sensitive nipple between his lips. His tongue explored it before taking the hardened bud fully into his mouth in delicious sucking movements. Repeating the erotic motion with the other breast, he heard her whimper.

His mouth drove her wild, causing her to beseech him to take her. Her hips pushed upward, thighs parting so he had easy access to her throbbing body. She was insane with desire, reaching down to help him enter in a rapturous mating that threatened to consume.

Brad's thrusting body drove her to the edge of consciousness in a frenzy of excitement, her fingers digging in his back. She was unaware of anything but the madness of his body possessing her with endless motion, each one driving her closer to oblivion. Fast then slow, in tantalizing strokes, they encouraged her response.

"Give, wife, give," he demanded, making her arch upward until she cried out.

"Release me. I . . . love you . . . oh!" Deep murmurs of incoherent love-words mingled with his as he took her mouth, his body shuddering in long spasmodic movements.

He rolled to his side, keeping her with him, his body still possessing hers.

"Stay . . . don't move. So good. So damn good inside you . . ."

Cradled in each other's arms, they lay satiated. Silence gave way to sounds of a plane flying low overhead. Brandy was stunned by their loving. She had been so absorbed in Brad, nothing was cognizant. Not sound, not time, not place.

Brad moved away from her, their limbs outstretched, relaxing in the aftermath of intense gratification. His hand lazily traced the swell of her breast, the skin sensitive from his mouth.

"I love you." One finger traced the rosy aureole that circled her nipple. His eyes stared, entranced, as it hardened. "Did I tell you how sexy the white patches on each breast, across your sassy little behind and lower tummy look against the rest of your golden body?"

Brandy stopped Brad's exploring fingertip as it slid over the contours of her body, lowering to the point of imminent intimacy. "No, you didn't." Her fingers reached to mingle in the sweat-dampened hairs curling on his broad chest. "Do you like them?" She leaned over to kiss his throat.

"They are a good guideline. Each being strategically located," he explained. "My God, you make love like an angel."

"Is that all you ever think of?"

"No. Right now I'm going to the shower and you with me." He picked her small warm body into his arms and carried her to his bathroom and the large built-in shower.

Later, refreshed from her shower, Brandy sat in the middle of their bed, toweling her shampooed hair dry. She flushed thinking of Brad's actions in the shower, admitting she had not objected, but even delighted, in his unexpected physical prowess.

She was wearing a black silk slip-style gown. It was cool and comfortable and, Brad told her, excitingly sensual.

Brad had gone to the kitchen to get a tray, prepared earlier by his housekeeper. They were both starving but too replete physically to venture from the house to his restaurant. The sun would be setting soon and the vast bedroom was shadowed in comfortable light.

Brandy laid the towel down and was brushing tangles from her hair in long even strokes when Brad entered. He carried a tray heaped with sandwiches; snacks to nibble on: delicious-looking frosted petits fours; and tall glasses filled with crushed ice, fresh tea, and lemon slices.

They ate in silence, each enjoying their impromptu picnic more than an elaborate meal. Brad sat in the bedside chair, watching indulgently as Brandy licked frosting from her sticky fingers after finishing her second petit four. He returned the tray to the kitchen, his velour robe loosely tied. It was his one courtesy to Brandy's modesty. He was amazed that she still flushed when he viewed her body or she looked at him. Uninhibited in bed, out of it she was still prudish.

In the bedroom he waited until she walked from the bathroom, her hair laying like a cloud of silk around her shoulders, her perfume causing a tremor to run up his spine. He walked to the bed and sat on the edge.

"Come to me."

Brandy went to Brad, sitting beside him, face touching his shoulder, hand lingering on his bared knee. She looked up when Brad placed his arm around her shoulder, holding her tenderly, his eyes lingering on her face.

"Do you want to know where I was the past few days?" He leaned forward, kissing her lips briefly.

"On a business trip, weren't you?" She took his hand, raised it to her lips, and turned up the palm to kiss it. He was so big, yet tender as possible to see he never hurt her.

"About you."

"Me?" She tightened up, her throat suddenly dry, dropping his hand to her lap, swallowing rapidly in an attempt to act calm.

"Yes, darling. I know everything now."

"Everything?" Her face paled, her slender back became ramrod stiff. She bowed her head as she held her hands together to still their trembling.

"Yes. I flew to Los Angeles, did some unobtrusive investigating, talked with some friends of yours." Brad watched as Brandy rose, walked to the other side of their bed, and sat down. She huddled against the headboard, lashes lowered to conceal her widened eyes from his piercing ones. She was speechless, afraid what she would hear next.

"I flew directly from Los Angeles to London, England. Ten hours of monotony. I had an idea by then what I would find, but I wanted proof. From London I drove to Aberdare, Wales, where I found adoption records for Mr. and Mrs. Daniel Harcourt of the United States of America. Four years earlier they adopted a day-old baby girl."

Brandy lay on the bed, tears brimming her eyes as she listened. Brad's voice was soft, filled with sympathy as he continued, each statement correct to the smallest detail.

"You and your husband lived in London for five months prior to the child's birth, while Daniel taught United States corporate law. One month after your daughter's birth you returned home, the colonel never suspecting it wasn't your natural child."

Dazed that Brad had been so thorough, Brandy whispered hesitantly, "Did—did you learn anything else?" Her eyes were filled with pain as past memories came flooding back to haunt her.

"Yes, my love. I know all about Daniel now. I talked with Charles Brislain. I like him, Brandy, but I knew immediately the reason for your platonic marriage."

Brad lay easily on the bed, leaning on one elbow, his

212

other hand cupping her face tenderly. "Daniel was gay, wasn't he?"

"Yes." Her brief reply was barely audible.

"Tell me about it, darling. There is no need to bottle up your secret anymore."

Brandy flung herself into Brad's arms, her words muffled against his broad chest as her years of anguish spilled forth.

"Oh, darling, it was so awful not being able to talk to anyone. It's been years now but I can feel each moment of insecurity as if it just happened."

He lay on his back, cradling her face to him, his arms rubbing her body in slow languorous strokes. He was torn apart by her anguished words. She was so young, totally unprepared for the complexities of life, but he knew the telling would release her from the torment.

"Godfather kept pressuring Daniel to marry, demanding really, that he carry on the family name. The older Daniel was, the more inflexible Godfather became. Daniel didn't know what to do. He loved his father despite the lack of outward affection, cared for me more than any woman he knew, and tried desperately to change."

Brad kissed her scented strands of hair, understanding her youthful dilemma.

"Daniel was always kind to me, Brad, treated me gently. I married him with stars in my eyes, unaware how soon they would change to tears. Our honeymoon was a disaster. Overnight I changed from a young innocent bride to a shocked, rejected wife. Daniel confessed the first night that he had been involved in a homosexual relationship with Charles Brislain for years. He—he never ever tried to make love to me."

Thank God for that, Brad thought, stroking her trembling shoulders.

"Godfather's health was bad. He had just had his first heart attack. It would have killed him to find out that his only son was a homosexual. He's a stubborn old man, Brad. Set in his ways and uncompromising. He falsely equates sexual preference with manliness. My entire marriage was a masquerade."

Brandy looked at Brad, his compassion filling her with inner peace. "I didn't know how to deal with it either. I felt rejected, unfeminine . . . not woman enough for him. It took me months to gain a sense of balance. But worst of all, I couldn't talk with a single soul."

"You can talk to me now. Always, about anything that troubles you." He kissed her lips lightly, letting her continue.

"Daniel begged me to keep his secret. He wasn't open like people are now. We attended social affairs, entertained often, and had many friends, and to my knowledge not one knew our marriage wasn't normal—other than Charles.

"Daniel spent most nights with Charles. I became despondent, lonely; I needed something to love. Daniel arranged to adopt a child, hearing through Charles about a young unmarried girl with his same coloring in Wales. By us living overseas for six months, Godfather never knew I hadn't given birth.

"Our daughter gave my life purpose. Daniel was an excellent father. Denise brought us closer together, but our life was always like that of brother and sister. We had no intimate moments."

"Good," Brad told her, knowing an intimate relationship would have been disastrous to both of them.

Brandy stroked Brad's chest, her hands sliding down to rest on his flat abdomen, exposed in the open robe. She met his gaze, a faint rose tinging her cheeks visible in the dim lamplight. "I had never seen a man undressed until—until that night you came to me in Las Vegas."

"My God, darling. My poor innocent baby. You really were asking for trouble."

A sudden feeling of unreasonable resentment filled him. Jealousy over the five years with Daniel . . . despite knowing he was never her lover. Anger over his deception.

He trailed his lips across her forehead, his voice a ragged moan. "Did you love him more than me?"

Brandy raised her head, slender fingers holding his lean face still. With trembling lips she kissed his mouth, their breath intermingling during her soft whisper.

"Didn't you realize, my darling husband? When I gave you my body, I gave you my untouched heart also."

Brandy's eyes were like windows to her soul, her love bared, face vulnerable when she leaned over him.

The weight of her caring crushed him, made him humble to her every need. With a satisfied groan Brad rose, hovering over her slim, responsive body. With deliberate intent his eyes held hers as he tugged the confining robe from his body. Next came her gown, slipped over her head in one swoop. The wondrous look of sensuous desire turned her haunting eyes to dark amber velvet.

"Wouldn't like to try for our first black-haired gray-eyed son now, would you?" she asked, playfully fluttering her eyelashes.

"You liked it, huh?" he teased, cupping her beneath him, her trembling limbs like satin against his hips.

"Hmm . . . husband. Liking is too mild a word for

215

anything you do to me." She clasped his back, excitement smoldering in the depths of her eyes as her glance held his.

He took her mouth with increasing hunger, letting the familiar tide of sensuality rise, knowing she would give him release.

"I'm glad we both had plenty of sleep last night." A roaring flame ignited inside his body, his hands touching each satin smooth breast before descending over her quivering abdomen, lowering still as she arched upward. Sliding, probing, stroking to bring her satisfaction.

"Hmm, that feels good. Er—why?" she purred seductively, trailing her hand over his steel-hard biceps, gripping them when he moved.

"Because when I mentioned we would make long, slow love the second time, I meant the whole night through." Brad bent down, his breath hot against her navel, his tongue circling in ever-widening circles, touching where his hands had been.

She felt her stomach somersault, her skin still sensitive from his vigorous lovemaking yet eager for more. Her heart was filled with peace. Brad's wisdom and compassionate understanding had freed her mind of the last vestiges of despair. His erotic forays driving her wild, she drew his head to her, wanting to kiss his strong mouth. "I think you have wonderful ideas, but I have one myself."

"What?" he teased, his mouth moving to her ear to probe it, watching her reaction with pleasure.

"Could we ride to our hill, watch the sun rise, and . . . ?"

"And?" He laughed, knowing she remembered their first ride when she had begged him to love her and he had refused.

"And . . . you know." She flushed, burrowing her head into his shoulder.

"Right, Brandy?"

"Right, Brad."

When You Want A Little More Than Romance—

Try A Candlelight Ecstasy!

Breathtaking sagas
of adventure
and
romance

VALERIE
VAYLE

From the bestselling author of
Loving, The Promise, *and **Palomino***

The RING

Danielle Steel

A DELL BOOK
$3.50   (17386-8)

A magnificent novel that spans this century's most dramatic years, *The Ring* is the unforgettable story of families driven apart by passion—and brought together by enduring compassion and love.

At your local bookstore or use this handy coupon for ordering:

Dell	**DELL BOOKS** **P.O. BOX 1000, PINEBROOK, N.J. 07058**

THE RING $3.50   (17386-8)

Please send me the above title. I am enclosing $_____
(please add 75¢ per copy to cover postage and handling). Send check or money order—no cash or C.O.D.'s. Please allow up to 8 weeks for shipment.

Mr/Mrs/Miss _____

Address _____

City _____ State/Zip _____

Danielle Steel
SUMMER'S END

author of *The Promise*
and *Season of Passion*

As the wife of handsome, successful, international lawyer Marc Edouard Duras, Deanna had a beautiful home, diamonds and elegant dinners. But her husband was traveling between the glamorous capitals of the business world, and all summer Deanna would be alone. Until Ben Thomas found her—and laughter and love took them both by surprise.

A Dell Book $3.50